# CRACKERS FOR THE LYCANTHROPE

# CRACKERS FOR THE LYCANTHROPE

ROBB HOFF

Hydra
Publications
Booth 34

ISBN: 978-1-937979-96-6

Hydra Publications

Goshen, Kentucky 40026

www.hydrapublications.com

*For beta reader and friend David Alexander: of all my books, this one was his favorite. May he rest in peace.*

# ACKNOWLEDGMENTS

Many people proved to be generously instrumental in the transcription of Crackers For The Lycanthrope from its manuscript form into the copy you now see before your very eyes.

Many of them are no longer with us, but some have persevered in this world.

They know who they are among the quick and the dead.

As for the forthcoming account itself, it was uncovered within the Big South Fork National River and Recreational Area in south-central Kentucky, where the depth and power of our natural world thrives in its foregone conclusion.

The original manuscript consisted of four notebooks that were found bundled together in a wrapping of aluminum foil. This package was recovered beneath an obscure, sandstone landmark roadside of Kentucky State Route 92, known in its locality as the One-Wagon-Wide Bridge.

As the name indicates, this so-called bridge is relatively narrow, being just some seven feet wide. Legend has it that two brothers attempted to cross it simultaneously in the opposite direction, but neither yielded in their wagon crossing. The collision that ensued forced both the brothers and their mules off the bridge to their deaths in the precipitous fall from each side of the bridge.

Perhaps the brother who fell to his death on the southern side tried to grab the ledge that juts from the cliff roughly twenty feet below the bridge. The ledge itself is narrower than the bridge above it and provides the last hope for an imminent casualty to avert fate in a fall down the sheer two-hundred-foot drop below.

Regardless of history and legend, this Last-Chance-Ledge (as it is known) is the site where the Crackers For The Lycanthrope manuscript package was retrieved. After its acquisition, the content of the notebooks was eventually, and faithfully, transcribed into electronic format. The title, Crackers For The Lycanthrope, has been extraneously assigned. Hopefully, the title is an apt signature for the story within the upcoming pages.

Likewise, the dates of the individual journal entries that comprise this book were extraneously supplied. The actual composition date could be inferred from the dates provided, but the legacy rendered within the travelogue is timeless and perhaps even prehistoric.

It is the dubious nature of this legacy that has compelled the copyright claimant of the text to register Crackers For The Lycanthrope as a work of fiction, rather than non-fiction historical account.

Whether the following is perceived as fiction or history, the entries nevertheless begin at the Red River Gorge scenic site in the area of the Daniel Boone National Forest that is southeast of Lexington, Kentucky.

## APRIL 13TH

## RED RIVER GORGE, KENTUCKY

The band is all here. Their thunderstorm wails all around me. What better prelude than this for a welcome home. The first squall was nasty enough to send me scrambling back to the campsite this morning and move my tent from the riverbank to this shelter beneath Moonshiner's Arch. From here, I watched the sky bruise from the greenish glow around the line of black cloud lumps as the squall chilled with its imminent arrival into the Gorge.

Both the ravine and the surrounding canopy of wilderness do impede the passage of most of the gale gusts to this fork of the Red River. But, still, I finally decided to zip myself within my tent to protect me from the onslaught of wind and rain that howled and pelted all around me.

If the storm should drop a swirling bomb in the form of a tornado, the arch itself should mostly shield me from whatever debris might be blown down hill.

There was the drummer at the flap. That lightning bolt detonated directly above the arch and lit the inside of the tent like a strobe flash. I hate to think that I've come all this way just to eat a fatal dish of high voltage. Nonetheless, it truly is exhilarating to be in the midst of one of these violent Kentucky spring storms again after so many years. I feel more alive now.

Mercy is random, especially as I write all of these words.

This violence all around me is actually a breath of fresh air for me. I've been driven virtually insane by the lack of sleep over the last year due to the most vicious nightmare that recurs exactly the same way every single night without fail. The terrifying assault on my subconscious happens within three hours after I've fallen asleep, which has made me so sleep deprived and delirious that I could no longer function in the world I knew and the home I had for the past several years in Rome, Italy.

I'm just glad that I wasn't on the roam when all of this blew in. If my wife could've had anything to do with it, I'd have been in the middle of an empty field when the storm hit, smoldering alive by now. This storm is euphony compared to the tirade she unleashed upon me when I called her collect from a payphone at the airport. I probably should've never called her, but I would rather have her wish me dead instead of forever wondering why I had left Rome.

Anyway, my wife never allowed me to fully explain my disappearance, not to imply there really was adequate justification for my actions. Nothing that I could've said would've deterred her from her wrath. She sentenced me to the shame of her eternal hatred. I accept my disgrace, which is really only hers to claim, as I am here in the Red River Gorge, where the life we shared together might as well just be more debris in the wake of this storm.

Our separation does deeply sadden me, though. I never sought to elicit her bitterness toward me. It was a magical journey that led me to her, and the love that we shared for the time we did will always be what I gauge as love in my heart. She can do what she wants with the legal aspects of that love, though. At least I didn't take the entirety of our bank savings with me. I left her half of it, which isn't much of a consolation since her share only amounts to an equivalent of one thousand dollars. At least she has the peak of her earning power ahead of her.

I felt guilty enough to leave her all of our savings, but I'd have never gotten off the ground. The cheapest airfare from da Vinci to Chicago and Lexington, Kentucky left me with a remainder of just seventy dollars.

From Lexington, I still had a long way to go to get where I'm going, which is what I remember as home. I'll have to walk there—home that is—from here. That'll be at least a three-day journey, depending on the obstacles I encounter on route.

At least I was able to reach the Red River Gorge much easier than expected. I was sure when I had landed in Lexington that I was about to embark upon a hellish ordeal. The lack of dollars had rendered me at the mercy of everything and everyone. Fortunately, I was given the gift of a reprieve by a total stranger.

I didn't have any available transport other than my own two feet when I left the terminal at Bluegrass Airport in Lexington. I had bought a road map of Kentucky to aid me in my journey and had the luxury of road signs and sunshine to illuminate the way. Still, I had at least one hundred miles between home and my feet.

By the time I reached Man o'War Boulevard at the airport entrance, I resigned myself to hitchhike. I stuck out my thumb, walking backwards along Highway 60. I only had to lug a carry-on bag, but even this pittance of remnant belongings became a burden. I had only hoped to hitch a ride to the other side of Lexington. When I saw the red pickup pull out of a hotel driveway and veer to the shoulder, I thought this hope had been realized.

What joy it was to watch the Confederate flag bumper sticker backing toward me, despite any misgivings I might have had about what the sticker represented or the person behind the wheel who displayed it on his truck bumper. I climbed into the cab after the driver answered that he could drive me to the other side of Lexington. I introduced myself to him–Virgil–before I revealed that my destination was where I am now–the Red River Gorge.

I thought serendipity had peaked when he offered to drive me as far as Winchester. This extra distance alone considerably shortened my journey. I thanked Virgil for the ride and offered some money to him. He waved off my offer, though, saying that he had to go to work in Winchester anyway. He then told me that he managed a sporting goods store. I felt further invigorated by the prospect that I'd be able to buy the supplies I would need here at the Gorge.

Virgil then probed into my circumstances. I stammered somewhat, unsure where to begin and how much to disclose about myself. I finally was able to spit out that I was returning from overseas and wanted to spend time in the Gorge before I decided to do anything else. I divulged two passports from the side pocket of my carry-on bag, one Italian and the other American. I then told him that I hadn't been in the United States in about ten years, ever since I had left my home in Kentucky for England. I also said that I had lived in Italy with my wife for the past several years but that we had decided to end our marriage.

I mentioned that I would eventually return to my home county farther south of the Gorge, but I had no family left there except for my old Grammy who I wanted to see before it was too late, if it wasn't already too late.

Virgil remained silent following my disclosure. His knotted brow seemed to indicate some suspicion about me, so I remarked about how comforting it was to see his shotguns mounted on the rack behind us. I told him that the only guns I had seen recently were the Uzis that the guards at da Vinci airport toted.

The topic of firearms instantly engaged Virgil in conversation. He started to run down the list of guns at the sporting goods store that he managed. I steered the conversation toward camping gear, as I talked about some of the supplies I remembered using before I left for England. Virgil then updated me on what he considered were the most significant developments in camping gear over the past decade.

But our talk did eventually shift to why I had returned to Kentucky. I pleasantly evaded as much as I could in my effort to redirect our conversation toward my upcoming visit to the Gorge. It was good that I did this because Virgil provided me with some vital information about the very place where I now camp–Moonshiner's Arch–a spot with a troubling history of shootouts and violent deaths.

This campsite is in what was once a controversial area. I remembered some of the history but listened to Virgil elaborate about the ownership issues involved with it. He then said the federal government finally purchased the land here along the Douglas Trail. It is now part of the Clifty Wilderness that is the eastern border of the Gorge.

Before I departed for England, the Douglas Trail and the North Fork of the Red River were privately owned. The trail was accessible, though, from the state route that circled the Gorge. Campers frequented this place, including me. I came here once before with my high school friend Herschel, who drove us here. I remember we had to pay a fee to park at the gravel lot that led to the trail.

Virgil informed me that now there was no longer a fee to park or camp along the river. He also mentioned that, despite the change of the trail's status from private to federal, the location of the trail wasn't listed on any of the public maps of the Gorge. Hopefully, that will help keep the trail off the beaten path while I'm here. I could use the seclusion for a while.

The relative isolation of my campsite is furthered by its distance from the main tourist attraction: Natural Bridge, which is located at the southwest corner of the Gorge while Moonshiner's Arch is in the Gorge's northeastern part.

Additionally, there aren't signs advertising the Douglas Trail, which became something of a landmark ever since the U.S. Supreme Court Justice–William O. Douglas for whom the trail is named–hiked it to help prevent the Gorge from being impounded into a lake.

I'm glad the Gorge was spared such a flooded fate, so I could be here now in my return, despite the storm outside still crashing down outside of my tent. It is a gorgeous place, if you will, and the river, which is really more of a creek, is apparently a more excellent place to fish than I remember. Virgil claimed that he had often fished this section of Red River and always left with enough fish of size to make it worth his while.

I was glad to hear Virgil say how good the fishing is here. With meager funds remaining, it made more sense for me to invest in a rod and reel than to try to hoard food or not eat at all for a while. I brought this up to Virgil–the fact that I had very limited funds with which to buy the survival supplies I would need for the Gorge.

When we finally reached the sporting goods store, we spent

much of his shift amidst the wares of the store, discussing what best suited my needs for my imminent camping experience. The store building itself enhanced the shopping experience for me. It was a log cabin, and, although my sense of history had been altered significantly by my immersion in the antiquity of Rome and Western Europe, the smell and construction of the cabin exuded age.

Virgil said the cabin was an old general store that had changed ownership several times since its construction over one hundred years ago. The musty aroma there did much to bolster my frame of mind with the excitement of my venture here to the Gorge. I have Virgil to thank for that. Without his intervention into my life for one solitary day, the Gorge might have swallowed me without so much as a sound. I could've been added to the count of those who perished here, some vanishing within the vastness of the Gorge never to be heard from again.

Now, here I am at the Red River Gorge in a tent beneath Moonshiner's Arch. Very much alive and equipped to meet the challenges ahead of me here, thanks to Virgil.

My benefactor continuously outdid himself with his hospitality. Once he realized just how limited my funds were, he offered to let me borrow a tent on consignment at the store for as long as I needed it. I wasn't at all put off by the fact that the tent was a clearly used, small single-man dome tent with a price tag of just twenty dollars. His gesture was so magnanimous in my estimation that the little dome tent might as well have been the mansion of tents because Virgil had granted me the most fundamental reprieve that I needed to meet the Gorge on its own terms.

I was nevertheless somewhat concerned when I did actually set the tent up here. I feared that the shock cord poles might splinter when I arched them. They didn't do that, and the grommets are still all intact. The tent even has a rain shield and stuff bag that holds the tent and all. I couldn't have asked for anything better suited for my purpose or easier to carry. The latter part of that function became even more important once I realized how loaded down that I would be with the other items I needed to make my trek to the Gorge.

I had to buy another bag just to carry all of the other stuff I bought. I had to put some items back because they wouldn't fit into the bag, which cost me five dollars by itself. I did buy a piezoelectric lighter, camper's toilet paper, water purifying tablets, utensil knife, and cooking supplies that included an enamel skillet and small, stainless steel pot. I also bought a can of cooking spray, canned meat, aluminum foil, and a five-pound bag of potatoes that the store featured as a camping sales special.

I forgot to buy a cup, but the collapsible five-gallon plastic container I bought has a nozzle from which I can drink. I also bought a four-inch lock blade knife.

I went somewhat overboard in my purchase of a two-piece fiberglass fly rod with a reel already spooled with fly line. The outfit was another consignment good and cost just fifteen dollars. I could have had an ultra-light spinning reel combo for less, but perhaps got caught up in the romanticism of the moment in my prospective return to nature. The fly rod and reel added even more expense, though, when I picked out the leader line, tippet material, and five wet flies, only to discover that these items put me over my seventy-dollar limit.

As I thought about what I could absolutely do without, Virgil extended another reprieve to me by offering a twenty-percent discount, including the purchase of the fly rod and reel. After he rang up the sale, took off the discount, then added sales tax, I had eight dollars and change left. I offered the money to Virgil, but he insisted that I keep it.

The objects of my attention thereafter surprised him. He said as much while I browsed the section of archery accessories. I explained to him that if I could find burning bush viburnum in the woods, I could temper the branches into a functional recurve bow and some relatively true-to-flight arrows. All that I would then need was a bowstring and some glue for whatever points I could fashion, or possibly buy. This evidently impressed Virgil because he then ushered me to a recurve bow from the consignment goods section.

I had thought he had just wanted to show me some function of the bow that I might replicate through some makeshift means, but Virgil said, instead, that the bow was his bow and mine to borrow if I wanted. I really thought I should decline his offer, but he wouldn't have offered the bow to me unless he really wanted me to have it. A price tag of fifty dollars dangled from its taut string. I would've offended him if I didn't accept his offer, so I graciously accepted the bow and thanked him with the enthusiasm and sincerity that is merited by such a gesture.

Still, I was overwhelmed. The bow had a sight and quiver already installed. Its draw weight was a comfortable fifty pounds. Before I could mention that a viburnum arrow might not fly from his bow, Virgil had already brought a four-pack of generic arrow brand to me. The arrows were the right length for me, and they were nocked.

The arrows cost six dollars and a package of field points cost another two. I gave the rest of my cash to Virgil. That's when he told me that he actually owned the store. I laughed.

The advantage of my misfortune in Rome began to dawn upon me. I would be rid of millions upon millions of people and all of the congestion and jabber that went with it. What's more, I wouldn't have to eat any more pasta (although I do wish I had a bottle of Barolo right about now), but, regardless, I might be able to eat healthier here at the Gorge than I had in Italy for the past several years.

Time will tell that, though. I haven't fly fished since I left Kentucky, and I'm liable to hook my own ear before I catch a fish. Virgil provided some refresher points about the art of it that I might try here. It was his recommendation to use flies that sink as opposed to dry flies that float.

I can't help but think that Virgil might envy me in my freedom in some way that made him want to help me even more. As the store owner, I realize he didn't exactly lose any money in helping me, but his kindness still seemed to me to be as genuine as it was large. When he offered to drive me from Winchester to the Gorge, I refused at first, telling him he had already gone above and beyond with his help.

But he insisted. I had convinced myself that I was prepared to pitch my tent wherever necessary on my way to the Gorge and trudge the remaining miles. I was tired, though, and it was uplifting to believe that it is possible to find a friend when one was needed most.

Still, I had my doubts. His Confederate flag bumper sticker kept crossing my mind. I even wondered if he might be setting me up for something else, like bludgeoning me to death then taking all of the sporting goods back to the store to resell.

But I dismissed that outlandish notion and any other ulterior motive that I might've imagined he had. So, away we went with me and my cobbled together survival gear in tow. I kept the conversation lively by telling tales of my life overseas, all of which he seemed to find entertaining. I appreciated what seemed to me to be his genuine concern for my fate, like he was a Samaritan ordained to be at the spot of my hitchhike as soon as it began. Whatever his views or beliefs, Virgil has my eternal gratitude for his brief, but critical, intervention into my life.

Before we parted ways yesterday, he gave his business card to me. He told me to call him if things didn't work out for me here at the Gorge or in my home county after I visited my old Grammy. He said he could put me into contact with a few employers and living arrangements were available in Lexington and Winchester for as little as twenty-five dollars per week.

I thanked Virgil again for all of his help, then I promised him that I would return his bow and the tent. He nodded and said that he would see me then. I watched his truck leave, thinking when I ended up working again and had some extra money, I'd buy all of my sporting goods from the store that Virgil owned. Seemed like the very least I could do. I vowed right then and there to be a loyal customer of his for life.

What's more, if things do work out at home, I'll keep in contact with him, just in case we both have a friend for life. Perhaps that's the reason I felt a strange sorrow when he left me there alone in the Gorge. I suddenly felt exactly like what he had called me during the drive from Winchester to the Gorge: a lone wolf.

As I plodded along the Douglas Trail through the darkening woods, I felt that lone wolf presence of mind, and something more: I felt like a lone wolf who had been spared by a conscientious hunter who wanted nothing more than to help a lone wolf survive in this wilderness. All of the dread about the uncertainty that I would face after my return from Rome has now vanished. I knew it last night. Part of me has always been here. I really am home again.

As soon as the storm clears, I'll have a closer look at the river. It was already swollen this morning, but I might be able to locate a good eddy with ambush points to fish in the swifter current, provided of course that I can make a cast. I've already eaten a bit of canned meat and some fried potatoes. There's plenty of both left, so it's not like I'm going to starve, at least not yet anyway. I wrapped the meat in aluminum foil, then wrapped the whole can in foil. It's chilly enough here for the meat to keep. I'll do my best to stretch it for a couple of days, in the event I don't fish the river. Right now, it's just too turbulent and muddy. I doubt I'd be able to safely or comfortably wade in it today.

I just hope that it doesn't get too much colder tonight. I shivered last night before I fell asleep. Those shivers are nothing, though, compared to the convulsions that seize me when my own screams from my nightmare jolt me from sleep. I had hoped that this would stop once I returned home, but this reprieve didn't turn out to be an exorcism of whatever it is that terrorizes me. At least, not last night.

# APRIL 15TH

## DOUGLAS TRAIL

I now have company here. My seclusion is over far too soon, and I'm doubly aggravated as much by these newcomers to the site as I am by the unfishable river conditions. The storms finally subsided, leaving cloudless blue sky in their wake. When I returned to the campsite I had before I sought shelter beneath Moonshiner's Arch, the company had yet to arrive.

I heard them first upon my return from a downriver hike. Then I saw their tent, which was pitched not even ten feet away from mine. I suppose that the proximity of their tent to mine is what perturbed me most. With all of this seemingly endless acreage of national forest, I just can't comprehend why anyone would opt to do this. They obviously don't value privacy or have any appreciation for appropriate spacing. I doubt it's their relatively young age alone that's behind their poor decision.

Perhaps it was just the girl's idea. She's much more of a woman than a girl, actually. I'm guessing she's in her early twenties. Anyway, when I approached the campsite in return from my hike, I heard her protest the advances of her male companion within the tent. That's what it had to be, because she was almost shouting for him to stop doing what he was doing and get off of her.

I heard her smack him, too. Their tent flap then unzipped, and she crawled out.

I must've been a gruesome sight. She reeled and nearly shrieked when our eyes met. I'm probably not the most handsome of men on my best day, and the patchy stubble on my unshaven face, as well as my soiled clothes and otherwise unwashed self, must've taken her by surprise.

But then she just gawked at me after she stepped back. That's when I realized that she had violet eyes, which I had never seen before. Maybe she wore contact lenses that colored her eyes, but as stunning as her eyes were, they couldn't stop my own eyes from drifting down to her high hips that hoisted the tight blue jeans clinging to her long, thin legs. It was then that I was as struck by her exquisite proportions as she must've been shocked by my untimely filth.

That's when I stumbled and splatted butt first in mud. After that, I really looked like something that had just crawled out from beneath a rock after a hibernation.

She giggled, then her boyfriend emerged from the tent. His cheek was blotched from where she had slapped him, but this didn't seem to faze him. He intruded upon the gape that she and I had shared together. As I struggled to regain my footing in the slick mud, he lunged toward me like he intended to embrace me, hailing me as his neighbor. That's when I knew he wasn't from around these parts. He introduced himself and his girlfriend, then divulged that both of them were students at a university north of Cincinnati.

He paused after that, as if to cue me to introduce myself,

but I remained dumbfounded by the circumstances and the beautiful young woman. After an awkward silence, he remarked about my muddied appearance.

I had half a mind to start raving like a lunatic just to get them to pick their tent up and leave, but then I thought of the kindness that Virgil had afforded to me. I decided to talk with them in the semblance of an affable manner.

Now, I don't know if I should've engaged in conversation with them. I couldn't camp beside them even if I liked them. My screams in the middle of the night would curdle their blood and perhaps even induce their incontinence. I really don't wish to frighten them with that, which is why I moved my tent back to Moonshiner's Arch. At least that way, I could tell them there was something wild in the woods if they rushed up to my tent to see what the noise was.

But I did linger with them for a while before I moved camp. I definitely would've moved camp, even if I didn't have a nocturnal outburst to guard against. The young man asked me to borrow three things that I didn't have, and he didn't seem to care too much for the presence of the recurve bow. I tried to reassure him that I had the bow so that I could kill game if so disposed, but that didn't seem to allay his obvious anxiety about the bow.

I then explained that I was roughing it and trying to use outdoor skills to procure food. I told them that I did have some other food in case the hunting and fishing didn't fare too well. Hopefully, that made me sound less like a fugitive or more like a typical recreational outdoorsman.

That seemed to put the girl at ease somewhat, but his nervousness didn't completely subside. He's probably gladder that I'm gone than I am. Now, he can pursue his girlfriend without the threat that I'll thwart his intentions. She looks like she could kick like a mule if she had to, so I have no doubt about her ability to fend for herself, not that she should have to do so.

One positive about my relocation from the campsite was the free "Last Supper" the guy cooked up for me before I left. I offered to add to the mix with some fried taters, but they preferred their potato chips. He was quite enthusiastic about the meal preparations. His girlfriend seemed wary about the whole thing, as though he might injure himself in the process of cooking. She actually clapped for him when he successfully ignited the propane camper's grill.

While she is an appreciably lovely young woman, she strikes me as a touch dimwitted, or at least out of place in these woods of the Gorge. She seems better suited for a shopping mall, from what I remember about those teenage magnets.

And speaking of magnets, she definitely has one that points me north, but, alas, this is a pursuit that I'm just not up for right now. I know better than to try to persuade her in this regard. I'm probably not much more than ten years older than her, but in my thirty years, I've chased enough women to know that this one would be like beating myself over the head with my enamel skillet, especially after I made such a grand entrance for her.

Besides that, I couldn't bear to hear her talk any more than absolutely necessary. Her nasally accent makes me cringe from the harshest sounds I think I've ever heard emanate from anyone. She also cackles when she laughs. I realize that, as much as I don't mind watching her strut her fine form around the campsite, I probably couldn't withstand more than five minutes of her company if she had to talk at all during that time.

I wouldn't want to vie for her affection, either. Her beau has gone to great troubles to take her on a truly cheap date, and he has her all to himself in the middle of nowhere for a week. He must've really pitched her on the beauty of the great outdoors to get her to agree to come to a place like this, where she and her violet eyes are clearly misplaced.

At any rate, they'll probably stumble upon me beneath Moonshiner's Arch at some point. I wouldn't object to eating some more of their bratwursts again, if they invite me to join them for another meal. I'd actually welcome such an invite if I can't catch some fish or shoot a squirrel with the bow. I'm out of canned ham, so I'd better do something for food soon.

At least I have a cup now. I took the one they filled for me at dinner. This will be their little contribution to my wilderness cause. I just hope I'm out of their earshot. Hate to see them get hurt in the dark, if my screams scare them enough to flee their campsite.

# APRIL 16TH

## THE GORGE-DOUGLAS TRAIL

I heard them below me yesterday. They've found Moonshiner's Arch. They didn't ascend to the top of the hill, but it's just a matter of time before they find me. I had wondered if my screams had frightened them away.

Nothing has changed within my nightmare. These few days at the Gorge have done nothing to exorcise it from my sleep. Perhaps if the nightmare varied, I'd feel like progress was being made. But it hasn't changed at all. It has remained exactly the same:

When it's time, I awake within the same dream. I am completely aware, even though I'm still soundly asleep and know it. I awake within my sleep because of the ache in my bones and a nausea that saps all of my strength. I struggle to drag myself from the bed within my dream, then I crawl across the cold, marble floor. When I reach the open window at the foot of the bed, I pull myself up until I can lean against the sill.

I shake all over from the exertion, then I repeatedly retch.

Nothing is disgorged, but the shock to my body pounds my heart to the extent that the blood churning through me deafens me as it races to my brain and bulges my neck with throbbing fury.

Still, I am able to turn my attention to the landscape beyond the open window. It is always the same out there. The entire valley is blanketed with snow. Beautiful glitter is everywhere beneath the ever-radiant full moon.

Everything sparkles, that is, except for one apparent drift of snow in the distance. This anomaly always juts from the ubiquity, and, when I see it, I am always surprised to find it there, like I've never seen it before. The dread comes next, flooding me with the recognition of what I must witness again and again and again.

The incongruous spot rectifies itself with the flap of enormous ivory wings that exacts the percussion of a lightning bolt through the open window. The camouflaged monstrosity reveals itself in its launch above the valley. The thunderous claps repeat with diminished report as the Nightmare Eagle soars along a course that entirely eclipses the moon and smothers the beautiful dazzle below in shadow. Only a soft glow escapes the silhouette until the beast veers in its glide and moonlight bursts forth again.

Somehow, the creature actually swerves behind the moon before it reemerges to rise and hover above the full moon in all of its brilliance. The glare from its albino eyes somehow even exceeds the intensity of moonlight, and it beams from some unblinking depth to stare within my own eyes until its blast of glaring sight starts to scorch my throat somehow.

I hack as I stand but dare not avert my eyes from the hovering beast.

Then, its awful talons open and extend. The beast drops

over and over again from the same starry night to seize the silvery pocked moon and thrust it below the horizon.

Darkness and silence follow. I grope for recourse, but nothing that I do has helped me elude what follows. Perhaps a plunge from my dream window might end the real terror. I don't know. As real as the dream seems in its recurrence, I fear that such desperation actually might deliver my corpse to the daylight, and, even then, I'm skeptical that the nightmare would be over.

Thus, I inevitably muster enough strength to remain standing at the window. I have come to accept that nothing can yield any refuge from the indefensible approach of the Nightmare Eagle.

The thud in the distant darkness signals its return. I savor a moment of calm before the muffled bang of its flapped wings rumbles briefly, then the same fright escalates without exception. The next percussion comes quickly. This subsequent boom rattles the raised window sash. Initially, it's a breeze that rushes into the room. I resign myself to death in sleep at this point because the whoosh thereafter roars, and the subsequent gust always upends me.

My head smacks the marble floor. I am dazed within my nightmare, but I always manage to kneel amidst the wake of surreal wind. I then stand again as the turbulence wanes. I delude myself with the hope that something will change after I stand, even if this means that the Nightmare Eagle will thrust its aquiline beak into my chest and rip my racing heart from my body.

I have to believe that some variance will occur, but so far none has. The whole building then quakes, and I clutch my chest to lessen its constriction from my own fear. There isn't any wind this time. I eventually recover enough to realize that the

Nightmare Eagle is now circling above me in the darkness at this point. I relax during this reprieve and breathe as deeply as I can. I then collect my composure enough to stoop and grope for the open window. I always reach the jambs and press my palms against them. I have even come to clutch them in fear because I soon remember how horrible what follows is about to become.

Soon enough, the next blast discharges. Plaster from the ceiling crumbles down upon me. Once again, though, the wind does not follow. The blast then repeats itself just as loudly and as damaging to the ceiling as the first time. And again, there is no wind despite the shock to the building.

It is then that I know that the Nightmare Eagle hovers, and I imagine it above me like it had been when it was poised above the full moon. Just when it seems like too much time has elapsed between detonations from the descent of those unseen wings, the explosion above precedes the fury that sweeps my feet from the floor. I claw against the sill as the wind stings my eyes, and I do manage to remain suspended above the marble floor as I hang on for dear life.

But then the impact of the recoil passes, and my feet thump in their return to the floor. When I reopen my eyes, I am always astonished by the residual vestige of the flash because it has somehow illuminated the entire valley beyond the open window. I gaze at the beauty beyond my reach. And I await the dreadful descent of the Nightmare Eagle into my view.

Those talons: they come as ominously as ever. Their luster gathers to a nearly blinding gleam, but I can't turn away from the talons as they lower into view. The pristine and massive breast then comes. It swells in its descent before my eyes. The wingspan of the beast exceeds the periphery of my sight obstructed by the building itself, but I am mesmerized by the bulge of flexed muscle beneath the arch of the beast's wings until the ivory of its hooked beak reveals its unearthly sheen. Its eyes are closed as it hovers outside of my window.

The squall from its beaten wings batters me with each flap, but I lurch without being toppled, just so that I can inflict the same horrible conclusion upon myself. Once the fiery breath of the beast singes my face, its eyes pop open to paralyze me with the crazed omniscience of its glare. I scream and cower in agony. I scream even louder as my fingertips slip from the sill.

And then my perspective shifts as bizarre as ever.

I perceive through the eyes of the beast.

I watch myself blown backwards across the room. The expanse of its vision, that is now my own, widens, and with this width, the light unbearably brightens everywhere. Nevertheless, I somehow manage to observe myself shriek and shake as my skin bleaches until its whiteness is that of the Nightmare Eagle.

I believe that my shrieks are finally what awaken me. Then the bizarre sensation that happens next is always the same, ever since the nightmarish recurrence began more than a year ago: I watch myself return to my body from the other side of the window. It's as though I am hurtled from the eyes of the Nightmare Eagle and somersault through the room until I connect with my waking body. I return to my senses chilled and soaked, then I retch as spasms seize my body. This painful awakening eventually leaves me breathless and numb.

The screams and my convulsions would also jolt my wife from her slumber. At first, she lavished me with comfort and concern. This changed as the nightmare persisted. Soon, she awoke annoyed, and then angered, by my outburst. By the end, she just pounded me with her fists when my screams jolted her from her sleep.

I managed to maintain a regular schedule for the first few months after the nightmare started. I would succumb to sleep around midnight, despite the certainty that I would be terrified into consciousness within three hours. I would remain awake after that, but I just could no longer function during the day after some months had passed.

Eventually, the lack of sleep took its toll. I would collapse when I came home from work, only to be terrified awake by the Nightmare Eagle three hours into sleep. My wife and I tried to subvert the inevitable once we realized that I couldn't remain asleep for more than three hours. She would wake me before then, and I would stay awake as long as I could before falling asleep again. We repeated the cycle as much as possible, but the irregular sleeping hours just seemed to make things worse in the end.

I soon became desperate for some semblance of normalcy. I started to nod off at work, which is not a good thing when you're on scaffolding stories up in the air. Medication didn't help, either. I decided I had to quit my job a couple of months ago, then it wasn't much longer before my wife finally gave up on me.

She should've expected me to leave. I absolutely had to leave, but I didn't really count on the Nightmare Eagle following me across the Atlantic. I had such high hopes that a return home would purge the terror from my mind. So much for that.

Who knows, though? Maybe I still will be able to shed this haunt. I'm not actually home yet. I have considerable mileage to traverse before I reach home. I haven't been where I spent my childhood since I left ten years ago. There won't be much of a homecoming reunion, though. The only relative of mine that still lives there is my old Grammy, provided that she still is alive. She's really my great-grandmother and has to be close to a hundred years old by now.

I'll find out about Grammy soon enough. Right now, I just want to try to get my bearings. Despite the nightmare, I do feel at ease here within the Gorge. My return to Kentucky is already feeling like a liberation from all of the drudgery and dispossession I felt in Rome for the past few years.

Strange, though, that my excursion through Western Europe is finally over. It's been a long decade. I went to London when I was eighteen, departing to attend an international college that was owned and operated by a school in the states. I did spend my freshman year at college, but I opted out of school after that so I could gadabout on extended stays in London, Amsterdam, Majorca, Paris, and Corfu before I settled in Rome and married the loveliest woman I have ever met. We were married for four years before the Nightmare Eagle arrived.

Then it was all over.

And now, here I am in Kentucky again.

Ready for my life to start over, I hope.

# APRIL 17TH

## THE DEVIL'S CHIMNEY

It was a haul to reach this place. It must've taken a few hours, and I'll have to leave soon if I want to reach my campsite before nightfall. I awoke before dawn, soaked and shivering from another harrowing visitation by the Nightmare Eagle.

As soon as there was enough daylight to make my way to the river, I left to fish. A decent meal does wonders for a hungry body. It is very near to ecstasy.

Of all the fish I could have taken with my fly, it was surprisingly a catfish. I had to backwind feverishly during the fight to keep my leader line from breaking. It finally came up gurgling its croak and looked as ugly as I remembered a catfish looked. When I hoisted its homely head from the water, I was delighted that it was a channel cat: about a two-pounder.

The fish was a chore to clean, though. I crushed its head with a rock before I started. I thought I had killed it, but after I cut its stomach open and yanked out the guts, the fish somehow managed to start thrashing its tail. There it was disemboweled and suffocated with its head caved in, and it had the gumption to fight to the bitter end.

Maybe that was just nerves, though. Regardless, I admire a creature that can survive out of its element as long as a catfish does. When I swallowed its meat, I deemed that the spirit of the fish nourished me as much as its body did.

Anyway, the arrival of the catfish into my skillet was even more of a task to accomplish than already mentioned. I decided to strip its skin from the meat instead of cooking the fish with the skin intact. I used my lock blade to puncture a hole into what was left of the fish's caved-in head, then I shoved one of my field-point fitted arrows through the head hole and into the ground. From there, I cut the skin behind the head and began the process of peeling the skin from the fish.

Once that was done, I severed the head, and washed the meat. I then stuffed the gutted stomach with boiled potato slices before I wrapped the clean fish in foil. I set the foiled fish in the skillet then put it on the fire and waited.

The steamed meat was delicious. I gulped purified water from the cup I had absconded, and I rejoiced at the luxury of digestion. There was more meat there than I should've eaten, but I ate it all anyway. I wanted to just go back to sleep after such a filling meal. The day was just too nice, though, to waste inside of a tent. Besides, I really wanted to make this trek to The Devil's Chimney, which is a rock formation high above the Gorge that the elements have carved from the crag around it so that it appears separated from the rest of the cliff like some kind of actual chimney.

The beauty of the Gorge unfolds before me from this height of what has to be at least three hundred feet. This view is a celebration of my senses that were so sorely plundered for the past several years by the ancient clutter and modern congestion of

Rome. Even the toll of recent dead posted on the sign behind me is a soothing sight. It's unfortunate that anyone would die at such a beautiful place, but the spirits of those fallen here cheer within this silence.

The gravity featured beyond the ledge of rock indeed beckons the onlooker to jump into the Gorge. It is a strange impulse, but it doesn't feel like a suicidal one. Obviously, the end result is suicidal, though, and it's the same result as it would be by accidentally plunging to death.

I just hope that some of those casualties at The Devil's Chimney, who jumped of their own volition to find their release from this earth in flight, did so without any inkling of despair in their hearts. I hope that what lured them to their demise was a distorted joy for the beauty surrounding them and the seemingly boundless freedom that the Gorge intimates.

I recall from my adolescence that most of the casualties here were declared accidents. Undoubtedly, most were. Still, I know of at least one who succumbed to the allure of this precipitous place. That would be my friend Herschel.

However, Herschel's leap was somewhat different. His disregard for his own life possessed a purpose beyond any that I've ever witnessed. Besides, not only did he survive, he wasn't even injured because he didn't actually fall.

I'll never forget Herschel's jump here. It seeps into my consciousness from time to time, especially so when I would be working several stories in the air on scaffolds. Herschel leapt on the eve of my departure for England a decade ago. He drove us to the Gorge, and we had hiked here to The Devil's Chimney.

Of all the attractions here at the Gorge, this site probably claims the most lives. The crevice behind it just gobbles those up who fail to reach the top. The danger isn't in the width of the crevice, though, because the span is just a few feet. The difficulty arises after the crevice is hurdled. This is due to the height of the chimney top, which is the height of a person higher than the rest of the rock beyond the crevice.

Most of those who died making the leap to the chimney probably didn't envision how they would scale the rock before they flung themselves to it. The ascent requires about a ten-foot run before the leap can be made, then it's a matter of good traction and timing. If the climber slips or loses momentum in the scale to the top, the climber dies in the drop into the crevice, which descends all of the way to the bottom of the Gorge. It's much easier to slip than it appears, too, because the rock toward the top is weather exposed sandstone. There's always the risk that any tenuous foothold will give way if sediment is displaced.

Herschel and I had scaled The Devil's Chimney a few times before we went there that last time. We never had any close calls, but we didn't even talk about scaling to the top that day. We were just content to sit upon the rock ledge beside the chimney and dangle our feet while we watched buzzards circle in their soar at eye-level.

That's all we did, that is, until Herschel did what he did:

Herschel smiled at me before he sprang to his feet and ran toward the side of The Devil's Chimney that was perpendicular to the scalable face of the rock formation. There didn't seem to be any way that someone could leap to that part of the chimney without falling. I shouted his name as I leaned over the Gorge to watch his fate unfold. I had no doubts that he would collide with rock then slide down the side, falling to his death.

But Herschel didn't fall. He landed on a narrow strip of a ledge that couldn't have been more than two feet wide. His feet were steadfast upon the ledge, even as his head knocked against the slanted rock. His arms flailed in circles as he groped for the balance that he somehow managed to gain, then he arched his back so that he could cling to the sloping rock pressed against his chest. He slid his feet along the strip of ledge, then stopped to shakily stoop over it.

I heard him yank something from the rock. I wondered what he was doing, but really wondered more how on earth he could possibly jump back to safety. Once he had regained his precarious stance, I asked him what in the hell he was doing.

Herschel wasn't much on talk. He answered me instead by showing me what he had uprooted: a violet that had grown through a chink in the rock ledge. He finally did ask me if I thought the violet were pretty. I nodded to him, then he told me that he would give the flower to Lucinda when he proposed to her—that is, if he could reach the safety of the ground where I sat.

Herschel didn't need to explain his action any further for me. I knew what he meant. This leap of faith wasn't just compelled by some foolhardy affection for Lucinda. He would've been quite content to live upon her love alone without risking his life in this way.

No. Herschel wanted the blessing of the Gorge itself that the life ahead of him with Lucinda was all that he truly would ever need and that he was right where he belonged.

And he wanted me to bear witness to all of this, so that I could confirm that the Gorge had granted his request that day through a language that only he and I understood.

As Heschel looked up at me from the ledge, he continued to hold the violet out for me to see. It was clear to me then, and now, why he insisted that we go to the Gorge that day. He knew that Lucinda and I had flung ourselves carnally upon each other on top of The Devil's Chimney when he had went to visit his brother in the Everglades. He had entrusted me to keep Lucinda company while he was gone. Had anyone else been with Lucinda the way I had, Herschel undoubtedly would've killed them and scattered their mortal remains throughout the Gorge.

I watched him place the violet in his pocket. I appreciated the scope of his friendship, but I couldn't really relish that dimension of our relationship for too long because I knew what Herschel was about to do.

And Herschel just up and did it, too.

It was like his leap down: no warning. He knew he wouldn't be able to reach the safety of the rock where I stood. I dropped to my stomach as I hung my head over the Gorge and reached for him. He reached for me with his extended right hand, and I leaned over the edge as far as I could while tenuously gripping a protruding rock with the fingertips of my other hand. If I hadn't been able to maintain my precarious grip on that thin jut of rock, we would've both plunged to our deaths because there was no way I would be able to let him go once he seized my hand.

I struggled to pull Herschel up until he could gain a hand-hold atop the cliff. He had proved his point to me. We walked back to the truck, wordless in a depth of meaning that very few people probably ever get to understand.

Herschel drove me to the Greater Cincinnati Airport the next day. I thought our goodbye was final then, but I did receive a letter in England from Herschel a couple of months later. He had proposed to Lucinda with his violet the very next day after I had flown across the Atlantic. The two had set a wedding date for the spring, and he sent an invitation, knowing that I wouldn't be there.

Herschel and I always maintained correspondence after that. I'd apprise him of my whereabouts during my extended stays in Western Europe, then we had a more consistent communication via air mail once I settled in Rome and married.

Herschel was the only person from home with whom I maintained contact while I was abroad.

That winter of my first year in England, Herschel actually called me with the information that Lucinda was pregnant. His voice quavered then, and my voice probably sounded even less confident when I congratulated him. At the time Lucinda and I were together at the top of The Devil's Chimney, Lucinda revealed to me that she had been taking birth control pills for over a year. Herschel had also confided that to me before then. Still, the news evoked doubt about the true identity of Lucinda's child because I had climaxed inside of her without protection.

In the late spring after their marriage, Herschel called once again, this time with news that Lucinda had delivered a healthy baby girl named Celeste. That was the last time I actually talked with Herschel, even though I had always informed him of my moves–until now. Herschel doesn't know that I'm here. I'm really not sure that we should see each other again after all of these years, but when I return home to the small town that is home for both of us, we're bound to bump into each other.

I suppose there's still time for me to change my mind. I don't really have to return home. There's nearly one hundred thousand acres around me where I could just vanish, living out my days in seclusion. I'd definitely have to hone my survival skills, but winters here are relatively moderate compared to farther north. The idea really sounds like a fun challenge at this point.

Regardless of what I decide, it soothes me just to be amidst all of this fresh air and scenery again. Writing this in English is also helping me to clear out the cobwebs that are hung in my mind from almost exclusively using a second language for so many years.

I really do feel liberated now from the life I lived in Rome. I can recall the difficulty I had in learning a second language for everyday use, and I had such a paper chase of legal documents before I married. I can remember the ordeal I had when I reported that I lost my American passport. I had to file a report with Rome police, then produce a copy of the police report about the loss to the U.S. Embassy in Rome so that I could get my passport reissued and renewed. I was worried that the renewal would be denied because the original passport had expired the year before. I worried needlessly, however, as I received another passport with a five-year extension.

The dual citizenship process was the real rigmarole, though. It might've been simplified if I had known what to do from the beginning, or if I had returned to America so that I could have handled the procedures from here. I couldn't do the latter, since return airfare would've wiped out the meager savings my wife and I had accumulated.

So, I initiated the process from Rome. I had written to my mother three separate times within three months, but each time my letter that asked her to send my birth certificate was not answered.

That's when I decided to send a letter to my great-grandmother's post office box to see if she knew where my mother was or my birth certificate. Grammy replied with the same response that she had made the only other time I had written to her: that she would see me when the time came for me to return home.

As a last resort, I had written to Herschel. I didn't specifically solicit his help, but, instead, I just detailed my predicament. Nevertheless, Herschel responded by sending my birth certificate and copy of a clean police record to me. I'm not sure if Herschel just wanted to help me, or if he only wanted to guarantee that I would remain in Rome and not return to Kentucky to disrupt his life with Lucinda. Whatever his motive, he informed me that he obtained the documentation through a friend of his working in state government at Frankfort, Kentucky.

Eventually, the Italian Ministry of Internal Affairs deemed me worthy of dual citizenship, but all of that does me little good right now. At the moment, I'm just another mammal at the Gorge that has to obey hunger and sleep.

Undoubtedly, my nocturnal screams have introduced me to some of the other denizens here. I just hope I haven't disturbed them too much.

I had best leave Devil's Chimney for now. I was leery about leaving all of my gear at Moonshiner's Arch. My camping neighbors might help themselves to some of my necessities if I'm gone for too long. I have a long hike ahead of me.

## APRIL 18TH

### MOONSHINER'S ARCH

I had walked almost to the end of the Douglas Trail before I climbed down to the Red River. I didn't want to be bothered by anyone while I fished, and I thought the pool I chose was sufficiently secluded. I didn't want to wade with my clothes on, either. I hadn't bathed since I arrived here. I had rinsed a change of clothes in the current, but I was itchy and grungy.

Besides, I could fish at the same time I was technically bathing. Made perfect sense to me. Virgil said that the winter had been an unseasonably warm one. So, too, was today–had to be in the eighty-degree range.

So, I disrobed and hustled into the water, which was still quite cold regardless of unseasonable warmth. The first surge of frigid, running current against my thighs almost forced me back out, but I fought the urge to retreat. The water soon reached my stomach, gradually feeling a little warmer or at least not so freezing cold.

I had looped the cord for the stuff bag around my neck to

use for creel in the event I caught some bass–largemouth, small-mouth, Kentucky, rock, white, whatever. It dangled against my chest. I soon gained enough clearance for my backcast to cover the entire pool. A boulder, which was about half the width of the river and twice as high as I am tall, jutted at the back of the pool. It obstructed my view of the noisy trespasser approaching. There wasn't much else for me to do, other than remain right where I stood with my lower body submerged. I cranked the noisy fly reel to forewarn the intruder of my presence. Shortly thereafter, the Girl from Ohio with the violet eyes appeared before me, clad in a scant purple bikini.

Her nasally greeting grated upon my ears. I stammered in reply as I gawked at her, but I did manage to grin before I averted her voluptuous curves and violet-eyed stare. I almost asked her about her boyfriend's whereabouts. I didn't want to alarm her, though. Instead, I said nothing as I continued to fish. She finally broke the silence between us, asking about my luck. I was in the middle of pulling slack and was about to answer her when I went ahead with my backcast.

I didn't blame her for her laughter. In fact, it relaxed me despite its blare. A fish had taken my fly on the backcast, causing me to stumble and splash toward the bank when I whirled to contend with the fish. I tried to maintain my balance, but I just crashed into the water instead. She had probably observed my bare ass by then, and undoubtedly more dangling down my front other than the tent stuff bag at my hairy chest.

She certainly got a sustained view of my backside as I turned it toward her in my wade back into deeper water. Anyway, I recovered at being caught so off-guard. I didn't look at her as I reeled in the fish, but I realized by the meager fight that the fish had to be quite small.

Her laughter had finally subsided until I landed the fish.

That's when she erupted into hysteria. The little bass wasn't even a fingerling more than a couple inches long. No doubt she thought I was the most ludicrous fisherman ever, to be so thoroughly upended by the virtual minnow I had hooked.

I told her that I fell because I tripped over a rock when I turned. Her laughter eased by that point, then she actually asked me if I were all right. As I was about to release the fish, she blurted that she would like to hold it. I couldn't think of any reason why not. She entered the current, squealing when the frigid water lapped her bare thighs. She squawked about how cold the water was as she made her way toward me, but she kept coming.

Once she had waded to my side, I tweezed the fish by its diminutive lip the best that I could with the tips of my index finger and thumb. I informed her that the little fish was a largemouth bass. I advised her to try to take the fish by the bottom lip instead of grabbing it around the body, which could compromise the mucous film that protects the fish from parasites and subject the fish to disease.

Our fingertips pressed as I transferred the fish to her. I was surprised by her short fingernails and their lack of polish. She cocked her head at different angles as she raised, then lowered, the fish in her viewing of it. That's when I noticed the glaze that circumscribed her violet eyes.

When she again asked me what kind of fish this was, I caught a whiff of her smoky breath. I cringed from disdain, but I didn't want to hold her dysfunctional short-term memory against her. I again identified the fish as a largemouth bass. I mentioned that she could return the fish to the water whenever she wished. She then twitched, as though the reminder that she indeed held a fish had startled her.

When she stooped to slide the fish into the water, it was

impossible for me not to fix upon the deep groove of cleavage between her ample breasts. When she straightened, I couldn't help but allow my eyes to drift to her thick, erect nipples poking against her bikini top.

That's when she blurted her question: did I steal her cup? I admitted I took it, then I resumed the process for making another cast of my fly. She asked me why I had stolen it in a tone that struck me as more curious than charged with rebuke. I met her violet eyes again. She had me hooked, so I began to explain my predicament. I told her that I had lived in Rome for the past several years and traveled through Western Europe, but that I had decided to leave all of that behind to return to my home in Kentucky.

This disclosure prompted her to tell me that she recently spent a ten-day tour with friends in Europe that included stays in Spain, London, and France. She professed her desire to return to Paris someday so that she could fully experience that "City of Love," as she called it.

I remember hearing old timers in the region say that a fisherman who catches many fish must be living right. I was starting to feel like one truly blessed fly fishing nudist about that time, but the splash of steps below the pool crushed my surging élan.

Her boyfriend stopped in front of the boulder, lifting his mirrored sunglasses to reveal his glazed eyes. He then lowered his glasses and greeted me as his "long-lost neighbor." I acknowledged his presence as I worked a loop of line into a longer backcast that soon inched above the slope of the bank behind me. He then inquired about my luck, but before I could answer, his girlfriend blurted that I had caught a small largemouth bass. She waded to his side, tiptoed to kiss him on the cheek, then she told him that the water was too cold and that she wanted to go back to the campsite.

As they stepped from the water to the bank, she stopped to turn and address me, inviting me to join them for dinner later if I liked. I told her I was going to try to catch something a little bigger than the first fish, but that I appreciated the offer. She giggled before she took his arm and they left, but she turned toward me one last time before they vanished from my view to smile and flash her violet eyes at me again.

Not long after they left, a perfectly placed cast next to a half-submerged rock produced a decent-sized fish. It was a Kentucky bass, which is a kind of natural offshoot of the large-mouth and smallmouth species of bass, known in other locales as a spotted bass. The Kentucky wasn't as big as the catfish I caught before. I put the fish in my stuff bag and left. The fish proved to be plenty big enough to fill my skillet and curb my hunger.

# APRIL 19TH

## MOONSHINER'S ARCH

In a way, even though I'm not twenty years old again, I might as well be. The only difference between me at twenty and now at thirty is that I'm just a little physically worse for wear. Other than that, I know as little about my future now as I did ten years ago. The rain has washed it all away. My slate is clean. I'm free again, at least until I fall asleep.

The nightmarish recurrence that afflicts me is definitely something different about me now than ten years ago. I've resigned myself to see where the nightmare leads, which for now is in the direct path of the Girl from Ohio and her violet eyes. She and her boyfriend found my campsite this afternoon and visited me for a spell. I was glad to have their company, especially hers, but even her boyfriend interested me today.

They are both juniors at their university in Ohio. They were together for their spring break earlier this month for a jaunt down to South Padre Island at the southernmost tip of Texas. They made it sound like such a delightful place that their description made me want to travel there someday. The girl then cast her violet eyes upon me and mentioned that she was returning to South Padre in July with some of her girlfriends. So, perhaps I really should make South Padre Island travel plans.

Who knows? We might not have to wait until then to meet each other alone. We might have that chance right here at the Gorge. She seems very interested in me.

But that will have to wait for now. Her boyfriend is still very much right here in between us, and to his credit, he was quite engaging today with his conversation. He's a political science major who is avidly interested in the legalization of marijuana in all of its uses. He even offered to share his "peace pipe" with me, but I declined. The two of them passed the pipe back and forth while he talked about the variety of uses for marijuana and hemp in their different forms in between his tokes of the pipe.

I was quite surprised to hear just how far the effort to legalize hemp and marijuana had come since I left for Europe a decade ago. I mean, I knew about some of the efforts, but the details of the concerted movement to revolutionize the marijuana landscape astounded me. When I left for England, the whole idea of marijuana legalization seemed hopelessly bogged down in the politics of morality. I can even remember hearing about times when government officials authorized massive Paraquat dumps on crops in the state and federal grounds just to try to eradicate as much illegal marijuana growing as possible.

As a kid, I never really understood the entire political scope of the effort to eradicate and perpetually outlaw marijuana, but I can still vividly recall the talking-tos by Grammy about where Herschel and I were forbidden to explore because those areas were purportedly rigged with all manner of dangerous traps, including even land mines.

Fortunately for Herschel and me, we had all of Grammy's

acreage to tromp through. That kept us plenty occupied whenever we wanted to explore woods. We knew where Grammy kept her hemp plants. We stayed away from there unless she asked us to help her ret the stalks in the pond, stook their straw, or hand brake the straw into fiber and hurds. She wouldn't allow us to shake the brake and separate the line and tow, though. She always baled the heads of line fiber by herself.

Grammy made us promise to her that we would never tell anyone about her hemp plants. I never understood why until we were told by visiting police officers at elementary school that growing hemp plants was illegal. I still believe that Grammy only grew the plants for the stalk fibers. Some select, trusted customers used to come by and buy the hemp rope she made. She also used a lot of the rope around her property.

Grammy might have been in the business of selling buds for smoking. I'm just not sure. She did give a substantial amount of cash to me before I left for England. I really thought most of that money came from the moonshine she distilled in the woods and bootlegged, though. I never did ask her if she also sold marijuana. I might ask her just that if I do indeed see her again.

Of course, I remember Grammy coming unhinged when I told her that the police visiting school said it was illegal to grow hemp. She wasn't mad at me at all. She was irate about the fact that government authorities had come to the school to try to have children volunteer information about the location of hemp plants and implicate people, even if they were in their own families.

Grammy looked like she was about to burst a blood vessel when she yelled about how the government ought not to be trying to fool a bunch of schoolchildren to snitch on their kin, regardless of the illegality of marijuana or if people around these parts were making bootleg money by selling it.

I understood Grammy's point in full context when I visited Amsterdam, Holland the first time and partook of marijuana sold in cafes there. The grounds for illegality of growing marijuana seemed discriminatory to me. If there were a market for people to smoke it, let others grow it to fulfill the demand.

But I also understood the hemp side of the equation because of Grammy's knowledge and the tradition of using the plant for productive means that had been passed down for generations. Grammy told me that Kentucky hemp was grown extensively for military purposes during the World Wars. She said that American paratroopers relied upon hemp parachutes and that her kin had grown hemp legally during the second World War when the Japanese had severed the U.S. hemp supply from the other countries of Asia.

I never questioned, or verified, what Grammy told me about hemp. I never needed to do so, any more than I needed to verify that the first United States flag made by Betsy Ross was comprised of hemp fiber. I had witnessed the use that Grammy made of the stalks. That was all I needed to know about it.

But for my camping neighbor here at the Gorge, that was a different story. He really had dedicated himself to an entire study of the plant and its uses. Some of what he said I had actually heard about in European countries, as well. Hemp paper probably is a much more environmentally friendly product than traditional paper. These Italian notebooks upon which I write are, in fact, comprised of hemp paper sheets. Hemp is legally grown in Italy for paper and cordage, and even for fabric. Why that shouldn't be the case here in the U.S. for so long lent credence to my camping neighbor's contention that certain industries suppressed hemp plant production through political pressure against any legislative effort to legalize it.

He was really specific about the details of his argument,

including the corporations that orchestrated the conspiracy for decades. And he said that Kentucky would have been among the richest states in America had hemp and marijuana been made legal. Actually, he phrased it a little differently, saying that all of the gold ever in Fort Knox was just a drop in the bucket compared to the potential wealth that legalized marijuana and hemp would bring the state.

He also called it sadly ironic that Kentucky could house the federal government's gold bullion and still remain one of the piss-poorest states in the Union, especially as it had–in his estimation–a treasure of one of the most lucrative natural resources ever known to mankind. He continued to explain that this boon of wealth wasn't just about the use of hemp for both medicinal and recreational marijuana and hemp fiber-related products. No. This collegian espoused a much more widespread use for hemp that I had heard about in London, Amsterdam, and Rome. It always sounded too simplified to me before, but the guy explained it with more conviction and detail than I ever heard.

I won't pretend to understand all of the technical analysis involved, but suffice to say, I got the gist: hemp can be burned and converted to industrial grade oil and coal. The oil can be used for fuel, and the coal can be used for power. What's more, all of the hemp conversion would make for the greenest of all green alternatives to other polluting sources of fuel and power. Then he held his finger up to his lips, like he was stating a secret.

As admittedly engaged as I was by his conversation, I nevertheless found it difficult not to find his girlfriend and her violet eyes infinitely more alluring. I still wanted to find out what she did to make her eyes violet, if in fact that really wasn't their natural color, or have a closer look to see if her extremely fair skin somehow reflected a violet illusion from her eyes.

She actually rolled those violet eyes of hers a couple of times during her boyfriend's marijuana/hemp oration. She even smiled solely at me from time to time. I strained not to stare at her too much, though. The last thing I need here is some kind of ridiculous ordeal over somebody's girlfriend.

I thought we were about to part company again, but her boyfriend blurted if he could borrow my fly rod for a while. My first reaction to his request was to decline it because I couldn't afford to have such an essential tool for my wilderness survival broken by some stoner. My second reaction flooded my judgement when the Girl from Ohio heaved her chest with a stretch and soft moan. I suppose I fancied that he would immerse himself with fishing for a couple of hours while I entertained his girlfriend.

He asked me to join him. I declined, saying I had some other sites I wanted to see before dark. He then more or less ordered his girlfriend to follow him to the river to fish with him. She actually glared at him for this, then her stare relented before she informed him that she didn't want to get wet and dirty by the river. She said she wanted to climb farther uphill from my Moonshiner's Arch campsite to see what was up there.

He remarked about the risk of wandering around alone. She shrugged, saying she would be just fine. I felt a stirring within me when he told her to have fun without him. I retrieved my fly rod and handed it to him. He took the gear then said he would return it after a while. He moved toward her, and she turned her head as she leaned into him, allowing him to kiss her only on her cheek.

She said goodbye to him and took one full step back from him. He paused as he gazed upon her, then I told him to just leave the gear next to my tent if I wasn't here at my campsite when he returned. At that point, she walked past the arch in the start of her climb up the hill ahead of her. She said goodbye to him again then half-waved to me. I nodded to her before I added my own goodbye to him, which prompted him to turn and face me.

He wished me goodbye, too, then thanked me for the use of the rod. I patted him on the back turning him in the downhill direction toward the river. I could hear her climbing the hill in the opposite direction. We both glanced back at her before he turned toward the river. He said he would see me soon, then he began his descent.

I watched him go as I continued to listen for her plodding steps uphill through the woods. I detected that she had stopped in her ascent, but I didn't turn around to see until her boyfriend had disappeared from my view. When I did turn around, she was waiting for my attention: her hands on her hips and a delicious grin smeared across her violet-eyed face. She then motioned for me to ascend to her, which I was about to do when I heard rocks misplaced below the arch and then the approaching steps.

Among other things, my heart dropped.

When I turned toward the source of the noise, I saw her boyfriend's head bob into my view. He half-hollered up to me that he had forgotten about a nature hike tour he and his girl-friend wanted to take. He thanked me anyway for my generosity with my fishing gear. I called to her, louder than I needed to as she was looking straight at me and not so far away, but I wanted to maintain the appearance for him that she had proceeded on her way without him.

She appeared visibly vexed by his return, then she answered me as she began her descent. The two of them rejoined me beneath Moonshiner's Arch. He reminded her about the hike. She said that she had forgotten but really didn't want to go for the hike anyway. He then propped the fly rod against the arch and said they could do something else together instead.

At that point, it was clear to me and her that he wasn't going to leave again without her. She softly sighed, changing her mind about the nature hike tour. She wanted to take it after all. He extended his hand for me to shake, which I did. He released my hand first, then he put his arm around her waist and guided her in the downhill direction.

They both said goodbye without any mention of a future visit. The missed opportunity to be alone with her rendered me forlorn on one hand but stimulated on the other because her interest in me makes me feel even more alive now and excited about my future beyond the Gorge.

It's growing darker now, though. Time for me to try to sleep for a few hours, and hopefully not wake up screaming from my nightmare again. As much as I'd rather have spent some time curled up with the Girl from Ohio, the end of this nightmare once and for all is really my top priority anyway. If I could only figure out how to end it.

# APRIL 20TH

## MOONSHINER'S ARCH

The nightmare terrified me from sleep before dawn. As soon as there was enough light, I roamed the woods with Virgil's bow until late morning. If I had only suspected that she would visit me alone, I would've waited for her. I found this note in the cup that I stole from her:

"Sorry I missed you. I really wanted to see you again. We're leaving today, so this is goodbye. If you come to Cincinnati this summer, call me. I'll meet you there. I really enjoyed your company. I would like to get to know you much better. I heard some kind of wildcat screaming in the middle of the night. It woke me up, and I thought of you. Take care of yourself."

She left her name and telephone number on the note, which is stuffed into my wallet for safekeeping. As unkempt and overall foul in appearance as I am right now, I'm unsure what exactly made me attractive to her. Maybe I seemed wild to her, like the Gorge itself. Hopefully I'll find out later in Cincinnati.

I must admit to myself that the titillation I feel from her does remind me of the circumstances that led me to meet my wife in Rome. Only instead of an encounter at the Moonshiner's Arch in the Red River Gorge of Kentucky, my wife and I first connected at the statue of Charlemagne on horseback outside of the Notre Dame Cathedral in Paris. I noticed my black-haired Italian beauty admiring the warhorse Tencendur upon which Charlemagne sat. She remarked to her friend in Italian-accented English about the fierce beauty of the horse, then her friend replied in what I recognized as a Cockney accent from my time in London.

I moseyed up to them, waiting for her friend to step away from her before I spoke in my cleanest, clearest American tour guide voice I could muster about how the coronation of Charlemagne as Holy Roman Emperor restored the papacy in Rome as a political entity after the Germanic invasions of Italy.

She turned toward me with such an absolutely anguished look that I immediately blushed. I stammered for some response that could rescue me from my failure. All I could come up with was something to the effect that his warhorse, Tencendur, was a fine stallion, and Roland told their tale well in the Song of Roland.

I then beseeched her with my eyes either to help me out or just walk away. That's when her brown eyes widened, her cheek dimpled, and she throatily laughed as she grabbed my forearm. I just grinned and nodded until her laughter subsided and she lowered her hand from my arm. That's when she asked me if I was being funny on purpose, but her pronunciation of the word "purpose" threw me off. I told her that Tencendur is a horse, not a porpoise like an ocean dolphin.

My future wife burst into such laughter at that point, that her English friend hurried to her side to see if something were wrong with her. I shrugged when her friend knotted her brow at me. Finally, my wife-to-be hugged my arm, pulling her face to my chest and looked up to me, smiling. She said Charlemagne might have been coronated the Holy Roman Emperor, but I was the funniest man she had ever met.

That worked for me at the time. One thing led to another, and she spent the rest of her holiday week exclusively with me. We spent considerable time together at the flat I shared with a French friend of mine. As much as I tried to consummate our newfound attraction to each other, she insisted on her vow to remain chaste until marriage. I stopped my seduction of her and decided to enjoy her company instead, holding hands, kissing, and hugging in between our conversations and touring around Paris. We remained in communication after she returned to Rome. She invited me to stay with her in her apartment for a couple of weeks. She worked four days a week, but we still were able to enjoy each other's company. I returned to Paris very much in love with her. After two more visits to Rome that year, I left for good to be with her. Our engagement followed within a couple months after that, and we were married within a year.

Honeymoon love swept us away in our first year of marriage. It was so much fun, and we were so happy. I felt like I had found my soulmate and "porpoise" on this earth. It seemed like everything that marriage was supposed to be.

Until we received the news that she couldn't have children. She was so devastated by this that I never allowed myself to think that she might have known of her infertility before we married. It just seemed like the tragedy to end all tragedies for her. I told her fertility treatment might work wonders in that regard. It took some time to pursue that...and a lot of money that we really didn't have at our disposal. As our debt mounted from not only that, but also our living expenses, we soon found ourselves entrenched in the battle that everyone seems forced to wage after a while–that of day-by-day financial survival.

Sadly, we stopped with our pursuit of fertility. After that, the physical passion between us just didn't work like it had before. Plus, I believe her religion compounded her inability to fully cope with our childless future. She ripped off Italian tirades that spewed about how our marriage was cursed and we weren't worthy of the blessings that others receive through holy matrimony.

Eventually, she turned bitter and even paranoid that I would leave her because she couldn't have a child to bond us together for life. Nothing I did seemed to quell that storm completely.

Then I started to experience a much more immediate problem of my own, a real curse that terrorized me then and now. I probably would have maintained my life with my wife in Rome because I truly loved her and wanted to help her restore her happiness for herself and us together. But the sheer fear that seized me every time I went to sleep became unbearable. My problem became me. There was, or is, as it now seems, no way to escape it.

Anyway, I left my wife in Rome. I have no intentions of going back. Maybe that will change if my nightmarish condition ends, but I really doubt that I'd go back even then. I needed a fresh start, regardless.

I had hoped that the Gorge would cleanse me. As beautiful as this wilderness is, I really thought that its depth and purity could exorcise this demonic force from my sleep. No such luck.

I'll have to leave the Gorge soon, I suppose, especially now that the Girl from Ohio has taken her violet eyes and supple curvaceousness away from me. Also, the appeal of this whole living-in-the-woods thing is starting to wear off for me. Too much like hard labor for me.

Besides, I really do want to see my old Grammy again. I just hope that she's still alive. I haven't tried to confirm that. Maybe Herschel can help me in my return home. Then again, I'm fearful that I permanently ruined our friendship when I ravished the love of his life ten years ago.

I'll have to be at the mercy of someone, though, when I leave the Gorge because I don't have a red cent to my name. I loathe the need for money. To me, it seems the more likely root of all evil than the love of it does. It messes the mind when times are so down and out that it seems impossible to function with any purpose other than a short tail of hope and vial of derangement.

I checked my billfold again. No money there, just a priceless note with a phone number and name that fills my breath with life. Let the Gorge eat the heart of time.

## APRIL 22ND

## HOME

She is not here. The chicken coop is in disrepair, and the neglected garden is now merely dirt choked with weeds. No signs of the hemp patch or still, but I didn't really expect Grammy to be involved with dope or moonshine at this stage of her life.

The cabin interior does suggest that she still lives her, or at least has lived here recently. The interior areas of the cabin that Grammy would frequent most are relatively dust free. Also, the potbelly stove has ashes, and there is coal inside, as well as some chopped wood outside.

I'm taking these as signs that she's still alive.

Now, the task is to locate her. I'd hate to think I missed the opportunity to see her again. I feel bad about not keeping in touch with her the past several years. Hopefully, she doesn't hate me for my neglect.

I think that Herschel would've written to me if Grammy had died, but she might have told him not to contact me if anything happened to her so that I wouldn't feel obliged to return. I suppose I'll have to visit Herschel and Lucinda to find out about Grammy.

There's really no point in guilt, but I'm remorseful that I didn't keep better track of Grammy over the years. I exclusively lived with her from age three through ten. After my father was killed in a car wreck, I was left with Grammy so that my mother could go to Florida to work. I grew up under Grammy's wing amidst the acreage of woods surrounding her cabin. She developed my mind during my formative years more than anyone else, plus I spent a lot of time in her woods and at her cabin during my teenage years.

The living conditions at Grammy's place didn't meet modern day standards, but that didn't mean I disliked how I lived with Grammy. I always loved drawing well water. I was quite content to do what she asked me to do. Besides, I spent most of my time roaming the woods. Staying in the cabin with no indoor plumbing or electricity just never seemed like a big deal to me, even after I started to go to school. Up until then, I probably thought that all little kids had a Grammy to make the outhouse seat smaller so that they didn't plop into the effluvium below.

The outhouse here is still as rank as ever, though. The mud daubers and flies populate its interior. It takes some daring to sit over the outhouse hole. I'd been stung by wasps before in the outhouse, but the worst pain that I ever received from an outhouse outing wasn't from a wasp sting. No, the cause of that pain resulted from my errant aim of urine stream as I stood over the hole. Grammy thrashed my bare behind with a switch for that one. Seemed she didn't want to have to sit in my pee when she tended to her own business.

I definitely improved my outhouse aim thereafter. I still received another thrashing after that, though, when she caught me messing around with the tubing coils of her still. That put an end to my curiosity about the unusual apparatus that produced her moonshine. I would ask questions, however, about the still and her moonshine production as I grew older. She always thwarted my inquiries. She didn't want me to carry on the family tradition, especially on her property.

I'll always admire that little old woman. She had to be in her late seventies when she raised me. She's the one who taught me how to read, too. She would, in fact, slavishly teach me how to read. I'm not sure when exactly she began her tutelage, but I do know that I was a proficient reader by the time I started kindergarten. This advanced education actually created a problem for me. The other kindergartners were terrified of me. They thought I was a raving lunatic because, not only was I literate, I also could recite dramatically without the typical Kentucky accent. I retained my notoriety for this peculiarity into high school. My flair for the intensely dramatic came to a head when I had a confrontation with Herschel over it.

But Grammy had prepared me for the kind of assault that Herschel would launch against me. After all, Grammy was the one responsible for my eccentricities in this regard, so she should have readied me for the antagonism I would face. As Grammy professed an undocumented claim of direct kinship with Edgar Allan Poe, her library consisted of his volumes alone, with the exception of a Great Depression era collegiate dictionary. I learned how to read by reading those works by Poe.

Furthermore, Grammy had me read aloud every day for extended periods of time. She taught me how to enunciate without a southeastern Kentucky accent, which she didn't have either. I suppose that the training in inflection and the nature of my reading material did make me quite the spectacle in my school classrooms.

And there was another trait of mine that catapulted me further into weirdness among my peers, as well as something of a behavioral problem for the teachers and administration during my elementary school years. I possessed a photographic memory: I could read an entire page once, then reread it in my mind for several hours afterwards. That in itself wasn't the problem, though. The problem stemmed from my misuse of this gift in the classroom, which made it difficult for my teachers to cope with me.

Whenever I felt bored, or otherwise so compelled, I would just start reciting passages from the works of Poe. These deliveries weren't mild ones. They were of the same seemingly deranged strain that I would employ whenever reciting Poe for Grammy. They were snarled and electric with all of the maddened delirium I could envision at the time in my child mind. I really wasn't trying to frighten anyone, but that's what happened.

There was one girl who would always start sobbing whenever I disrupted class with my dramatic readings: that was Lucinda—the same Lucinda who would later marry Herschel.

And it was Herschel who did something that the school administration wouldn't do in regard to my outbursts. Sure, the teachers would often send me out of the classroom to the principal's office. It became quite customary for me to sit in one of the offices and read from a book they provided, written by someone other than Edgar Allan Poe. I can remember reading a part of a dictionary that went into lengthy detail about etiquette. I had to read that section several times, in fact.

But Herschel's reaction to one of my fits gave me more pause than anything I read in the school administration offices. Fortunately, Grammy had prepared me for Herschel's aggression. She had fashioned a punching bag out of hemp stuffed with chicken feathers. When she wasn't improving my reading skills, she taught me boxing techniques. I learned how to hook, jab, and move as I threw punches.

Grammy also used to play a game with me that she called "Get Away" in which the object was for me to escape before she could smack the back of my head. Of course, Grammy wouldn't always tell me we were playing the game, and I would bear the brunt of a full, open-handed whack to my skull before I realized we were playing. This game of hers actually readied me for games that we played a lot in school: *Kill the Man with the Ball* and *King of the Hill*. I enjoyed playing these games, and probably played them as well as I read.

Despite all of the training that Grammy had provided, and even the skills I developed by playing rough physical games at school, I still wasn't quite prepared for Herschel's action in the third grade, I believe is when it was. Herschel wasn't playing a game, and by the time I realized that, I had suffered a busted lip and the loss of four baby teeth.

I must've been stunned by the punches because I still don't clearly remember what happened after that. I do recall how it ended, though. Herschel was trying to squeeze me to death. The teacher finally intervened, but I had bloodied Herschel's nose and gashed his throat with my teeth. He must've belted me in the jaw and the side of my head because both were swollen, and my ear rang on that side of my head where he hit me.

For some reason, Herschel and I became best friends after our fight. We became inseparable after that. I would later discover that Herschel had some specialized training in the art of self-defense at home, too. He was big and strong for his age, but his older brothers dwarfed him. They had trained Herschel through their meanness. If Herschel didn't learn his lessons, he wound up bloodied and bruised.

Despite Herschel's attempt to quiet me and our subsequent friendship, I continued my outburst of Edgar Allan Poe recitations. I mentioned them to Grammy, but she never discouraged me. Surely, school administration had notified her about them, too. Maybe she just didn't want me to stop reading at the cabin. I know she enjoyed my readings as much as I did. She often would cackle with delight while I read.

However, my life would change quite a bit after my mother returned from Florida. She rented a house in town, and I was forced to live with her, although I was permitted to stay at Grammy's on the weekends. Sad as I was at first, I admit I did rejoice at times from the basic amenities that were now at my fingertips and just a flush away, too. I indulged in the hot water and found myself fascinated by the telephone.

Besides all of that new stuff, I now was also a neighbor of my best buddy Herschel, who lived just down the street. The two of us often loitered in town when we weren't playing neighborhood games with other kids or exploring the woods behind Herschel's house on our own. We always liked the woods best, even after Herschel's brothers told us stories about deranged wild animals and a wicked witch that lived in the woods. I think they just told us that junk to keep us from finding the treehouse fort they had built.

We were actually at their fort one day when we were shocked by the same sight, but for different reasons. When Herschel saw Grammy emerge from the thickness of woods, he thought she was the evil witch about which his brothers had warned. Of course, I knew better, but I couldn't say anything to keep Herschel from screaming, crying, and running away from her as fast as his feet could take him.

Grammy and I both had us a good laugh about that. I ran to her and hugged her. It seemed like it had been a while since I had last seen her. The most interesting thing about her visit, though, was that she had blazed a trail for me from the fort site to her woods, which actually bordered the woods behind Herschel's house. I went with Grammy on the trail that day, all the way to a place that I recognized within her woods. She made it easier for me to keep track of the trail by hanging loops of hemp rope along the way. She pointed those out to me then, and, later over the years, Herschel and I would look for them until we mastered our way through the woods to her property.

Unfortunately, the track through the woods took a couple of hours. I actually returned home that first day just before dark, but that didn't alarm my mother because it was normal for me during the summer. Grammy did advise me not to tell my mother about the trail through the woods, though. When I asked Grammy why, she just said it was better not to make my mother worry about me. The round trip journey was so long that Herschel and I could only take it during summer months when we were off of school and the days were longest.

The summers during middle school grades were the best for our travels to Grammy's woods. We would often camp overnight near Grammy's cabin, sometimes for a couple days and nights in a row. Grammy would take care of us, and sometimes even take us hunting. She had an old muzzleloader that she used. I never fired that heavy thing, despite Grammy's persistence to get me to do so.

Then during one of our visits, Grammy presented brand new 20-gauge shotguns to Herschel and me. She kept them at her cabin, so we could only fire them when we came to visit. At first, we could only shoot under her supervision, but soon Herschel and I were exploring the woods with our shotguns in hand.

The frequency of our outings to Grammy's diminished

more and more as Herschel and I continued through high school. I started to work when I was sixteen. My mother bought a ten-speed bike for me, and I used that to get to my job. I worked for a sporting goods distributor full-time for both summers, but just part-time during the school year.

Herschel also started to work when he was sixteen. He worked at a fuel station, and he would save enough money to buy an old pickup truck during the summer before our senior year. He spent most of his time with Lucinda, but the three of us did frequent the Gorge together, even if it were only for day trips. Oftentimes there would be four of us to make the trip to the Gorge, including my date, who was usually a different girl each time. The truck bed had a camper top, so my date and I rode there.

By then, I had already been accepted to attend college abroad in England. I didn't have any qualms about letting my dates know that I had no intentions of sticking around after high school. A few of my dates couldn't care less beyond the couple of hours we spent together alone having our way with each other, but other dates just didn't want to involve themselves with me because, presumably, I would be leaving for good. I didn't ask those latter dates to make any more road trips with us to the Gorge.

Of course, the one-day trip to the Gorge that was most memorable for me is the only one I wish I could take back: the outing Lucinda and I had while Herschel visited his brother in Florida. At the time, I couldn't really dwell on it because I was getting geared up to leave the country for school. I received a partial scholarship and a federal grant to pay for school. I had also saved up over two thousand dollars, which Grammy matched with her moonshine and hemp money. I was extremely grateful for Grammy's help, but also for my mother's contribution to my cause. She was hardly in a financial position to help me much, but she nevertheless set enough money aside to buy one-way airfare for me to England.

One-way seemed right, too. I don't think anyone I knew ever expected me to return, but here I am again.

Oh. I suppose I should write down how I physically returned home from the Gorge. My old buddy Virgil from Winchester showed up yesterday at Moonshiner's Arch in the Gorge. He was curious to see how I was faring out in the wilderness with the supplies I had got from him at his store. I confessed to him that I was about ready to pack in the whole back-to-nature thing.

I suppose I would have made it home eventually if I had made the trek from the Gorge on foot, but there's no telling how much of an ordeal that would have been. Thanks to Virgil and his pickup truck, I returned home the easy way. When he asked me if I wanted a lift, I could barely contain my relief. I told him he was saving me a trip to return his recurve bow to him, but he said I should keep it because I "wasn't really out of the woods yet."

## APRIL 23RD

### GRAMMY'S CABIN

The racket of a cardinal at dawn awoke me before the Nightmare Eagle could terrorize me with its horrific flight. Once I realized that I was spared by the little bird, I pondered how shrill the vibrant songbird can blast its welcome of daylight infusion into a world of darkness.

Now, that's it's midmorning, I'm reminded just how annoying the bird is when it won't stop its incessant noise. But still, the male cardinal is a thing of beauty in its brilliant red that juts like a Christmas bow from all of this surrounding greenery. And why? It really does seem like the male cardinal is so colorful just to divert any raptor attention from the female garbed in dun contrast.

Wow, there's a female now. She has joined him, quieting him with her arrival next to him. There, he just launched with her following him into the canopy of these welcoming woods.

Grammy always claimed that the sight of a cardinal was a harbinger of a visitor. It's obviously untrue, but it seems apropos at this point since I hope that Grammy will return here soon.

As I sit here, I'm struck by the memory of something that Herschel and I saw in the woods when we were in our early teens. We had camped overnight in the woods when a howl erupted close to us at our campsite. It jolted both of us wide awake, and we barely made eye contact before each of us scrambled for our respective shotgun. Herschel said to stand back-to-back so that we could cover all directions in case we were attacked by the source of the howl.

I had never seen a wolf in the wild here before, and I don't remember hearing about them still being here, either. But what I saw was a wolf, snarling in the distance, yet unwilling to come any closer to us. Before I could even take aim, the wolf bolted into the darkness of the woods. I asked Herschel if he saw it, but he said he hadn't.

It now seems strange to me in retrospect what Grammy said to Herschel and me after we shared our experience and I told her that I saw an actual wolf. She made us promise that we wouldn't shoot it if we ever saw it again because the wolf would never harm us. Those were her words. How she could say that with such certainty troubled me now more than it did when she said it, I suppose. I mean, how could she possibly know that such a beast wouldn't harm us?

Maybe all that Grammy meant was that the wolf was such a hunted creature, driven into virtual extinction, that any survivors wouldn't risk contact with people under any circumstances.

Perhaps I'll ask her what she meant by that, if she can even remember saying what she did about the wolf that I only saw. That is, of course, if Grammy ever does return here.

# APRIL 24TH

## THE WOODS

I t's never enough to know that wretchedness just descends over and over again. I can't believe who I am and what I've done. This latest heap of self-inflicted misery sickens me to my soul.

I was more hopeful than anything when I started out into the woods this morning for my hike to reach Herschel's childhood home. Grammy's enduring loops of hemp rope guided me to as much pleasure as anguish. The presence of the loops themselves made me quite glad. Such a familiar sight on such a familiar path made me feel at home again, indeed. I can even envision Grammy tiptoeing to tie the loops to branches with enough room in the knots to allow for a decade of tree growth.

In retrospect, it sure does seem to me now that Grammy spent a lot of time taking care of me and trying to make sure I could find my way back to her if I ever needed her. I am ashamed that I haven't reciprocated her regard for me in a way that truly benefited her. Now, I'm ready for my love for her to be at her disposal alone without any regard for myself or my future.

Nothing that I can do for her in her remaining days upon this earth could be as generous and compassionate as what Herschel already has done for her, though. He was there when she needed someone to help her the most, not me her great-grandson or my mother, her granddaughter. We were the only two direct descendants left who could've taken care of Grammy, but neither of us were here for her.

Without Herschel to drive Grammy to the hospital for her treatments and help her recover from them, I doubt she would've lasted as long as she has. He drove her for her surgeries, her radiation, and her chemotherapy, and he made sure she was as comfortable as possible afterwards. He bought her whatever she needed to make her life easier, and he was her biggest advocate when she needed to convince the medical people that she shouldn't be permitted to die just because of her advanced age. He made sure everyone he needed to talk to about her understood that Grammy intended to fight for every last breath she could get.

I certainly expect that Herschel will continue to act upon his concern for Grammy, regardless of my presence. Clearly, he's been more of a grandson to her than I ever have been. Herschel's altruistic heart further vexes my own treacherous one because I'm wrought with the guilt of having defiled his beloved during the debauched fling I initiated with Lucinda.

Once again initiated, I should say.

What a way to repay Herschel for all of his kindness to Grammy while I was gone. I'm such a degenerate. I never intended for this to happen.

But all of it did happen.

When I reached Herschel's childhood home, I went brain-dead at the sight of Lucinda opening the screen door. But then I got straightened out right quick as she stood there full-bosomed in her skin-tight halter top to complement her even more skin-tight short-shorts.

My God, I swear she's the hottest woman I've ever seen, even when she was a teenager and a little bit gangly in comparison to the voluptuously proportioned woman she is today. Still, I could've resisted the temptation. It wasn't like Lucinda opened the door ready for me to bend her over in her living room, but she made it hard—literally—when she hugged me like I was the second coming of whatever she had been missing her whole life.

She released me, though, and brought me into the kitchen to sit at the table. Sitting helped me cope with my libidinous surge, especially with most of Lucinda concealed as she sat opposite me at the table. I thought my desire for her would pass even more when she related Grammy's misery to me and described all that Herschel had done to help Grammy.

I thought I was out of the woods then.

Until Lucinda invited me—out of the blue—to join her in her bedroom. I asked her why she wanted to go into the bedroom. She stood from the table and point blank told me that her and Herschel were estranged but still living together in the house. She added that the time I ravished her at The Devils Chimney was so much better than any sex she ever had with Herschel.

I declined her offer, at first, and suggested that we needed to find out more about Grammy. That's when she said Herschel was staying in Lexington with Grammy for another night while Grammy awaited another doctor's visit.

Then Lucinda disclosed that her daughter, Celeste, wasn't Herschel's daughter. No, she was mine. What's more, Herschel knows it, too. She said he even wants to put Celeste up for adoption if Lucinda wants Herschel and herself to try to be man and wife again.

Before I could even respond, Lucinda said that she'd much rather have a go at her and I living together as man and wife, even if we didn't get married. That way we could finish what we started all those years ago atop The Devil's Chimney and raise Celeste together. She even suggested we take off soon for some other place in some other state for a fresh start away from all of the turmoil here.

I told her I absolutely could not do that. I had to be with Grammy, but when Lucinda broke down in tears, I knew I was in deep trouble. I really did try to console her at first, telling her how sorry I was for causing all of her problems in her life. My tenderness was genuine. My touch was a gesture for healing. Even when I stroked her hair, it was with the affection of remembering how wavy, bronze, and soft it was. And when she pulled herself to me, guiding my hand to her thigh, I still thought that our embrace was one of commiseration and hope for an improved tomorrow.

But I was hard as a rock, and it didn't take long for her to feel her way around to find out just how hard.

Her glacial blue eyes dilated when I turned her to grip her petite waist. We embraced again, closer, tighter, and longer. I knew it was hopeless then. We had re-ignited our animal passion for each other. What followed left both of us basking in the afterglow of extreme sexual exertion with repeatedly orgasmic results in virtually every room and hallway in her and Herschel's house.

Once again, intimacy with Lucinda was the most intensely satisfying sex I ever had, even topping our tryst atop The Devil's Chimney those ten years ago. Both of us trembled from our exhaustion until we gradually came down from our rapturous height. That's when we really started to talk to each other.

And the buzzkill of our sexual high together started to set in.

Grammy's condition was much worse than I imagined. She has been deemed terminally ill for a few years now, yet she has persevered despite her gloomy diagnosis. I learned that, since my wedding in Rome, Grammy has undergone a double mastectomy, and had one of her legs amputated. What is probably even worse for Grammy is that she is blind.

Despite her affliction and these handicaps, Grammy has nevertheless managed to fend for herself for the most part. She obviously doesn't live the way she used to live, but she still doesn't require continuous care. Lucinda said that Herschel has visited Grammy at least twice a week since he first drove her to the hospital in Lexington a few years back.

I just hope the sight of me doesn't startle Grammy the rest of the way to death. It infuriates me that she is being tortured to death like this from a physical perspective, but what makes me want to bawl is the triumph of her inexorable will as she extracts as much life from her depleted body as possible. There must be a glimmer of hope for her to cling to yet. Otherwise, she would have given up the ghost by now.

The unbridled lust between Lucinda and me might have been for the best, provided it got my gnawing energy out of my system for a while. I just don't want my pursuit of sexual appetite to distract me from the attention I'm going to give to Grammy for the remainder of her days.

It's true that I might have to deal with distraction, and perhaps even hostility by Herschel for what I and his wife have done together. Plus, Lucinda might prove insistent about her claim that Celeste is my daughter and not Herschel's. The whole adoption suggestion really doesn't sound like Herschel, but we'll see. I can understand why Herschel might harbor considerable resentment for harboring a child that wasn't his. Celeste must be a constant reminder of the betrayal Lucinda and I committed atop The Devil's Chimney.

Lucinda does seem concerned about Celeste's welfare, but her conversation suggests that her real concern is about how she will manage to care for Celeste and herself financially. That will have to all come out in the wash if Lucinda and Herschel decide to divorce.

As for me, I can't even begin to have any kind of feelings for Celeste, but that might all change once I actually meet her. Who knows? Lucinda and I obviously share an intense physical attraction with each other. Maybe that will develop into full-fledged relationship with our daughter as the centerpiece of a life we might decide to live together as a family.

Lucinda doesn't want to wait, though. She wants us to go off together right now, and I told her that I just can't do that. She then said that she wanted us to pick up Celeste from her grand-parents' house so that we could spend time together before Herschel's return. But, again, I told her that I had to get ready for Grammy's return.

My reaction displeased Lucinda. She pulled away from our repose to sit at the edge of her bed. After a prolonged sigh, she stood, stating that we needed to cover our tracks in the house as best as possible. She stood and turned toward me with her fists wedged against her hips, telling me that I should leave and return tomorrow night when Herschel would be at the house.

I told her I wasn't going to leave just yet. Her physical endowment overcame me again. I rolled myself to the edge of the bed then sat in front of her. She maintained her posture with her fists against her hips and a frigid countenance until I pushed her fists from her hips and grabbed her around her waist, pulling her to me, and then onto me so that she could straddle me as we once again engaged each other.

There would be no covering of tracks for a couple more hours after that, just more mess made. Once we had finished our physical exertion, Lucinda made turkey breast sandwiches and heated leftovers. She gawked at me more than once, while I devoured the food. I made sure to take a few more sandwiches for my hike back through the woods.

I finally left Lucinda, although I can't help but crave her flesh even as I write this now. I returned to Grammy's cabin and grabbed this notebook. I really had no idea what I was doing with it as I started to follow the path of hemp rope loops back to Lucinda. I made it to what's left of the old fort in the woods, then sat to write all of this.

Twilight is descending now. I best return to Grammy's cabin before I do something I'll regret.

# APRIL 25TH

## GRAMMY'S WOODS

Her lips are blue. A few strands of coarse hair form a clump upon her otherwise barren scalp. Her face has shrunk. Deep furrows contort the crusted flesh there. Busted blood vessels purpled her leathery cheeks.

The hinges of the heavy door creaked when I entered the cabin. Grammy sat at the kitchen table, which is the same cable spool that has always been situated there. Grammy wheezed through a grimace. Her nostrils flared when she croaked her question, "Who's there?" Her dead, glazed eyes stared at me. Before I had managed to say that I was in the kitchen with her, her toothless grin scrunched her face even more. She tried to stand. Her bony arms shook as she strained to push herself to a stance. She couldn't stand, though, then she plopped back into the chair and slumped against the cable spool. Her back heaved as her little pink tongue slid past her thin blue lips with each wheeze she made.

I knelt beside Grammy and caressed her hunched back until her belabored breathing eased. She tried to breathe but could only belch rancid fumes. I used the most soothing tone of voice I could manage when I told her that I was going to stay with her and help take care of her.

She shook her head no repeatedly before she made a quivering motion with her hand to indicate that she wanted to write something. She then pointed to the counter stand next to the kitchen basin. I retrieved the note pad and pencil from the stand then brought them to her. I guided the pencil into her claw of a grip. Her blank eyes glared dead across the room as she scrawled her message to me on the pad. She stopped when she broke the pencil lead.

Grammy wrote this: "Get Away!" I told her that I would never leave her again. I gently embraced her fragile remnant body as I crouched beside her. She tried to shove me away from her, so I released her and straightened to a stance beside her. I watched her grope beneath the cable spool table. She divulged her antique revolver, pointing its barrel toward my stomach as her hooked fingertip searched for the trigger. I noticed that the hammer was already cocked, so I silently stepped from her aim.

Grammy gurgled something before she fired the first shot where I had just stood. Her arm jerked behind her from the recoil, but she somehow had maintained her grip on the gun. I don't have any idea why she would try to kill me. She must be senile or hateful about my prolonged absence.

I really didn't have time to ask her anything at that point. She struggled to cock the hammer again. By the time I heard it click, it was too late for me to try to disarm her. I lurched for the door. When I reached the door, she fired her gun. The bullet must've hit the wall as I flung the door open and leapt to the porch. I didn't look back when I jumped from the porch. I sprinted for my campsite in the woods.

When I reached my tent, I squatted beside it so I could

remain within view of the cabin. Grammy emerged from the cabin shortly after I reached my tent. She hopped along the porch boards until she reached the top of the steps. She stopped there, then she scooted herself forward upon her sole foot. I don't really know how she managed to do it, but she actually hopped down the steps. She kept on hopping until she neared the woods. She once again aimed her revolver, but not close to my direction. She then fired.

I didn't budge while Grammy just stood there on her one leg, as if she were waiting to hear me stir in the woods. She then tried to talk, but all that I could hear from her were unintelligible croaks, except for her last shout, which I heard ever so clearly: "Get Away!"

Finally, she turned around and hopped toward the porch. She grabbed the handrail to help her climb the steps. As much as I really wanted to help her in her ascent, I didn't for fear of being shot.

There's probably about an hour or so of daylight left. I've pretty much stayed in the same spot for a few hours now. I thought about visiting Herschel, but I decided against it. I'm about out of water, and I haven't eaten anything since this morning.

I suppose that I'll have to disarm Grammy eventually. I might have to find her other firearms, too, and take them. I hadn't bargained for this. I don't expect much sleep tonight. If I sleep too long, my nightmare screams undoubtedly will reveal my location to Grammy. I really can't imagine her hopping all the way out here in the dark just to shoot at me again.

I'm amazed by how far she was able to hop the first time. The spirit of this little old woman enlivens me, even as she imposes a very real threat to my physical well-being. I just hope

I somehow can convince her to stop shooting at me. I really want to be with her now, but she's making it virtually impossible for me to stay.

# APRIL 28TH

## GRAMMY'S CABIN

This is tenuous recourse to grasp what has happened. These last couple of nights and days have proven far too bizarre and inexplicable for me. These words are the legacy of the doomed. There is only the tale soon forgotten by the few who ever knew. There is the promise of oblivion, but far too much dread until then.

The best that I can do is survive while I wait this out. Grammy is about as dead as a live person can be, and I'm not sure if I should seek medical attention for my gashed arm. As much as it throbs and will likely result in infection, I think I'll just gut it out.

I've dwelled upon the possibilities long enough to try to stay focused upon what is real. But the evidence is starting to point toward my imminent ruin. I'd gladly return to my nightmare now if I could avoid what is happening to me while I'm awake.

The last time that my nightmare jolted me awake was just a couple of nights ago, but it already seems like an eternity ago. My heart had regained a bearable beat that night the Nightmare

Eagle visited last. I awoke, panting and soaked with sweat inside of my tent.

Then came the visible nudge against my tent from the outside. I watched in horror as the nudge repeated, this time pushing the tent plastic farther in. I crawled to the intruder and smacked the tent. That's when I heard the growl. At first, I was relieved, thinking that this was just a stray dog nosing around.

But then I was puzzled by the progress that it made upon its paws. It sounded like the creature was hopping away from me. I then heard it whimper as it plodded farther from the tent. I thought it would be safe to unzip the tent to see the creature, which to me looked like a large dog with a missing back leg in the unobstructed full moon moonlight.

I crawled out of the tent and stood. The creature turned toward me. It was a gray wolf, like the one I had encountered all of those years ago in the woods here.

Like the one Grammy had advised me never to shoot.

It hopped away as fast as it could. I pursued it. I heard it clamber through undergrowth and followed its path deeper into the darkened woods. When it finally stopped to turn and growl at me, I froze. We had reached enough of a clearing that the wolf could charge me if it wanted, albeit in its own hobbled way. I might not reach a tree to climb in time to avoid the wolf's charge, but I didn't doubt that I could dodge the handicapped beast if need be.

I just didn't want to harm it. I decided not to move as it slinked toward me. But when it did come close enough to lunge for me, I changed my mind and backed away from the creature until I finally reached a tree that I climbed. The wolf then turned and hobbled away from me. I should've returned to my campsite. Instead, I decided to pursue the wolf once again.

This time the wolf led me through the woods for what

must've been hours. I didn't realize the path was merely a sweeping circle back to Grammy's cabin until the pursuit of the beast led me to the old smokehouse behind the cabin. It then hopped at full speed across the cabin yard. I now jogged after it. It turned the corner to the cabin. I heard its claws clack against the porch steps before I turned the corner in time to see the wolf hop across the porch and nudge the ajar door open enough to enter the cabin.

I awaited Grammy's strained screams as I pondered how to drive the beast away from her, but no noise came from the cabin interior. I searched the porch for any kind of makeshift weapon I could find, but a cardinal startled me with its shrill greeting of the gathering dawn. Before I could resume my search for a weapon, I noticed the flash of a lantern light inside of the cabin. I cautiously guided the door open until the lantern glow revealed Grammy robed and seated beside the cable spool table. Her whole body shook as she struggled to lift her eyes in my direction.

I shouted for her to point to the wolf, but Grammy turned away from me to grope for the handle of the pantry door behind her. She pulled the door open then guided her trembling hand to a box on the middle shelf. The box shook in her grip as she brought it to the tabletop in the lantern light.

It was a box of crackers.

I turned from Grammy to survey the interior of the cabin. I again shouted for her to tell me where the wolf was. She only groaned, instead, in her frantic attempt to open the box of crackers.

But before Grammy could open the box, she fell to the floor, convulsing and retching as I hurried to her. I knelt beside her, then I slid my arms beneath her, scooping her frail, light body from the floor. She gurgled and shook as she pointed toward the box on the table. I gently returned her to her chair. She lunged for the box of crackers, tearing at the box top until she opened the box. She then plunged her small skeletal hand into the box.

When she pulled a handful of the oyster crackers from the box, several scattered across the tabletop. She tried to cram the rest into her toothless mouth, but only about half of the crackers in her hand made it to her mouth. The rest of them dropped to the table.

Grammy moaned softly as she sucked the crackers and her mouth puckered back and forth. She finally tried to swallow her mouthful of crackers but grimaced as she gulped repeatedly. She smacked her thin lips before she again plunged her hand into the box.

This time, however, Grammy groaned as she held the crackers in front of her. She opened her palm and brought the fingers of her other hand to feel the crackers. I briefly turned from her once again to see if I could spot the creature that had entered the cabin, only to have my attention redirected to her when she flung the crackers across the tabletop.

Grammy recoiled from the table and gripped her throat as she gurgled and groaned. I leaned toward her to see if she was choking, but then she released her throat and shakily pointed to the table. I looked to the crackers strewn across the surface.

Then I noticed the movement beneath the lantern light. The maggoty sight sickened me. Grubs of some kind had infested the crackers.

Grammy bumped against me when she fell from her seat. She gagged until she disgorged what she had ingested. Her whole body jerked as she retched horribly. I squatted beside her to lift her hairless head from her vomit. I then knelt and held her head against my lap. Her spasms continued even after she no longer retched.

Finally, the violence to her little body ceased.

She wheezed as she panted, pressing her bony cheek against my thigh. I stroked her leathery scalp and tried to comfort her by saying that the worst was over now. I told her that I was going to lower her head so that I could bring some water to her from her jug.

But she lifted her face from my leg and squinted at me with her blazing blind eyes. Her toothless gums gleamed within the lantern glow. As I wondered why it appeared that she could now see, Grammy lunged for my arm with her mouth. She clamped down on my forearm so hard that the clench of her bony gums actually hurt.

At first, I thought she was doing this to counteract her agony, then I felt the puncture of my flesh. I screamed from as much pain as surprise as I groped along her head for something to grab to pull her mouth from my arm. I finally yanked her head backwards repeatedly to free my bitten arm. I could feel its flesh tearing away. In the horror of the sight of blood spilling from my arm, I could see that Grammy's eyes were all white and blood oozed from her trembling lips. She finally just collapsed to the floor, seemingly unconscious.

I couldn't believe the condition of my arm, but I still maintained Grammy as the priority of my concern. Even now, she remains in far worse condition than me. Her breathing is scarcely perceptible, and she seems to have slipped into some kind of catatonia now.

I cleaned my wound the best that I could in her basin with what remained from her jug of water. The wound has become increasingly more painful, though. It throbs from the knot that has formed on my forearm. I have no idea how the puncture happened. I even looked into Grammy's mouth to see if she had any back teeth, but she doesn't.

At least she didn't bite the arm I write with, and I didn't need to fend off a wolf because it never reappeared. Where the wolf went, I can only speculate based upon my arm.

I suppose I should've already hiked to Herschel's house. Maybe he could drive both Grammy and me to the hospital. I'm noticing that the skin around my bite wound is starting to blotch purple. I suppose I could contract tetanus, rabies, or something worse. If the condition of my arm further deteriorates, I'll have to seek medical treatment, but I'm not sure I can explain the bite.

Despite the hideous sequence of events last night and the anxiety since then, one benefit resulted—the Nightmare Eagle is gone. However, I did awake within my sleep last night, and this consciousness within my dream began exactly like the nightmare had all those countless times before. The nightmare even reached the point where I crawl across the marble floor one last time then reach the open window to cast my gaze upon the same snowy valley that sparkled beneath the ever-radiant full moon of the nightmare. The apparent drift of snow in the distance is exactly the same, in the exact same spot, and does the exact same thing.

But before the behemoth Nightmare Eagle could flap itself into flight within my dream, I did something different: I jumped out of the window. I then clambered through the deep snow of my dream, straining to reach the beast as fast as I could on all fours. When I did reach the eagle, just as it was about to lift itself free, I pounced its breast, clawing at it and tearing its flesh with my teeth. The blood flowed and spurted all over the ivory beast and the snow. The Nightmare Eagle squawked its scream and flailed in its attempt to pry me from its flesh with its talons.

But I remained beyond its reach. I tore deeper into its flesh, crazed by the battering of its heart as I clawed and chewed my way to it. I clung to the inside of its chest when the eagle collapsed, then I found its heart and tore at it over and over again, its blood washing over me as I wolfed pieces of its heart in my frenzy to feed.

My motive for doing this, though, bothers me now. As I try to fully relive that dream moment, I have to confess to myself that my blood-thirst for the flesh of the Nightmare Eagle compelled my leap, not desperation to escape the torment of my recurrent nightmare.

Once I actually attacked the beast, my power possessed me with this deranged urge to devour the power of the beast itself, not just its flesh and blood. It seemed to me like I was engaged in a battle for survival, which I refused to lose.

And it looks like I really did win. I gorged myself upon the beast until the satiation of my blood-thirst rendered me asleep within my dream. I slept so soundly and long that, when I finally did awake, it took me some time to recognize where I was and why. I slept for several hours straight for the first time in a long time. I never felt so refreshed.

I certainly hope this serene slumber continues, but as much as a reprieve as it is, I'm unable to fully rejoice over how welcome its return is. The swerve of circumstances still placed me very squarely in the crosshairs of forces that could very well prove to be my undoing.

My arm is filled with a bane about which I dread to specu-late. Plus, I fear for Grammy's life for her sake and mine. I want her to remain alive so we can reunite in earnest, and I can show her the affection that I've been so sorely devoid in showing her for all these years that have passed.

And I also want her to live so that she can tell me why she bit me and what in the hell is happening to me now because of it.

## APRIL 29TH

### GRAMMY'S CABIN

Grammy revived this morning. After three days without food, she had to have been at the verge of death. I tended to her the best that I could, checking her pulse and breathing. I also dripped water into her mouth to hydrate her as much as I could, but she never responded in her comatose condition. When she finally did regain consciousness, I was relieved that she was still very much alive. Now I can do more to help her. I was amazed by just how alert she was after suffering such a physical ordeal like she had.

I drew water from the well for her, and she gulped a whole cup of it down without pause. She still doesn't have much of an appetite, though. She did reluctantly slurp spoonfuls of wheat cream porridge that I heated over campfire. I helped myself to some of that mixture, too, which I hadn't eaten in quite a long time and forgot was a staple in Grammy's cupboard.

It wasn't until the middle of the afternoon when she really wanted something more to eat, but she wouldn't have anything other than oyster crackers despite my attempts to heat some canned soup for her. I made sure to open the box and sift through the crackers to ensure there were no larvae or other foreign material. I had already disposed of the other box of crackers from which Grammy unfortunately had sampled some of the numerous grubs contained therein.

Despite the fact that Grammy did eat a couple dozen oyster crackers, I can't help but to think that she may require intravenous feeding before much longer. I admire her resiliency and hardcore tenacity, but another episode like the one she had probably would do her in for good. I suppose that I'll just stay by her side while she recovers on her own, though, at least for a few more days or until Herschel shows up with a better idea.

Grammy does have enough energy to want to get out of bed. I convinced her to remain in bed and repositioned her so that she can sit with her back against the headboard. She's nonetheless aggravated by her inertia. I suspect that, if I left her alone for a while, she'd get up and start hopping around again.

When I had visited Lucinda, she informed me that Grammy had trouble with speech due to radiation treatment, but I still barraged Grammy with questions, starting with why she had chomped onto my arm and how she had managed to puncture my flesh without any teeth. I also wanted to know if she knew about the maimed wolf, and if she had seen it enter the cabin, where the wolf had gone.

I also very much wanted to know how to treat the wound that she had inflicted upon me, but Grammy just kept pointing to her throat and croaking in reply. She finally made a writing motion for me to bring a notepad and pencil to her so that she could write her responses. I retrieved this very notebook for her, then she started to scrawl in the middle of one of the remaining pages. She printed a brief and barely legible message:

"Stay here kin. You are my heir."

Her scribble gave me considerable pause, but before I could dwell upon all of the implications of such a message, I beseeched her to elaborate. Grammy wouldn't go into any further detail, though. I suppose I'll just have to wait her out for that. Until then, I'm encumbered by both dread and anticipation. I'd rather view her message in light of her benevolent history with me, and not our recent interaction in which she shot at me and bit my arm. I don't want any more of that.

It definitely does cross my mind that Grammy might bequeath her property to me when she finally does die. A financial rescue like that could be a most welcomed reprieve for me. I'd really rather not think in those terms at all. I really am here to be with her. I never pretended or professed to want what she owns. She's the only truly important person remaining in my life. I want to share her remaining time here on this earth with her and experience her triumph in living the most life her worn out body can take. Her spirit inspires me to persevere as a mere matter of principle, and I will do whatever I can to help her survive, regardless of the agony it causes her because she clearly wants to stay alive.

Grammy rests now. The potbelly stove has made the cabin too warm, given the outside temperature, so I've had to open the two windows she has. The air flow has instilled some coolness in her bedroom. Now that she is resting, I've been able to write all of this. This leisure time for me to collect myself does, indeed, make me ponder my future. I'm unsure what I can do with these slivers and shards of what I once was. It'd probably be better for me to focus upon what might materialize here in the very near future.

Sooner or later, that will mean a visit with Herschel. He's bound to arrive here, or I might just decide to make the hike through the woods to his house. Of course, the latter could get out of hand again. If Lucinda should be there alone when I arrive, all bets are off. I just can't keep my body off of hers and vice versa.

I suppose that I should be grateful for the return of deep sleep and just bide my time here in this relative sanctuary. I awoke within my dream again last night to find myself snugly situated among the rocks below a slab of natural bridge. I'm on a ledge that seems to be some kind of den for me in my dream. Beyond the ledge is a precipitous drop into a gorge. I lowered my head and returned to sleep within the dream. Everything is so peaceful now when I sleep.

Now that my sleep is restored, perhaps I can also restore peace in my life while I'm awake. That would be most welcome, and it gets me to thinking. I doubt that Lucinda told Herschel about our latest tryst. If she had, I expect that Herschel would have already come to pay me a little visit here at Grammy's cabin by now. Of course, Herschel might've been more pissed with her than me. If that's the case, I just hope he didn't harm her. The Herschel I know wouldn't lay a finger on Lucinda, though. All the more reason for me to feel all the guiltier for having done what I did with his wife, regardless if they're no longer really together or not.

But then there's this whole adoption issue with Celeste, at least according to Lucinda. If I really am Celeste's biological father and Herschel has discovered this latest rendezvous between Lucinda and me, then maybe he's left or forced Celeste and Lucinda to leave the house. Either way, though, I would expect for Lucinda and Celeste to show up here at Grammy's.

I suppose I'll be drawn further into this intrigue about Celeste's true identity. I'm not sure how it can be avoided unless I decide to just leave without a trace, but I'm not going to do that. I'm going to stay here and see what unfolds. I must admit that my interest is somewhat piqued to ponder what life Lucinda and I might have together with our daughter. I'd just hate to steal another man's wife, especially when that man is my oldest, closest thing to a friend I know.

I'll have to leave that one on the burner for now. I best focus my attention on this bite that seems to have infected my arm. I'm no expert on gangrene, but the discoloration spreading around this bite has me wondering if I ought not to seek out someone who might know something more about gangrene and flesh bites than I do. The knot that formed at the point of the bite has hardened and darkened in color. My forearm is stiff enough to limit its mobility as the swelling has spread around my elbow.

At least I can still write with my good hand.

# MAY 1ST

## GRAMMY'S WOODS

The insects have gathered. Only a few mosquitoes have proven impervious to the repellent that I've smeared along the exposed parts of my body. I didn't use any of the spray upon my festering forearm, though. The mosquitoes don't appear interested in the infected blood beneath the boils of pus anyway. Perhaps, the hydrogen peroxide that I frequently pour on the wound deters the mosquitoes.

The flies are a different matter. Fortunately, only a few stragglers have taken notice of my arm wound. I've taken some pleasure in killing those that think they have found a juicy spot on my arm only to have their guts swatted out of them with Grammy's fly swatter.

After I lanced the excrescence upon my forearm with my lock blade, the pungent fumes and ooze of pus and infected blood still made me retch. I used the rest of the hydrogen peroxide I found in Grammy's cabin to flush the discharge. The wound undoubtedly is too far neglected for peroxide to have any real benefit.

I'm also now flush with fever and weak with nausea. I suppose delirium is next. The only positive about Grammy's bite is that I've lost all appetite. Even Grammy ate more than I did today, which is a good thing because there isn't much left for either of us to eat now.

Until the inevitable ultimately overwhelms me, I really don't have much other recourse than to console myself with plans and speculation. If I assume that I will survive my predicament, then perhaps I will in reality. At least my sleep remains as sweet as it's ever been.

I really need a car or truck so I can start to work my way back to some kind of financial solvency. I'd rather not rely upon anyone else for that, but I'm definitely at a crossroads on foot. Part of me wants to take the direction that leads as far away from this place as possible, while another part of me definitely likes it here in the woods without all of the garbage that comes with living in the festering open sore of a metropolitan area.

Of course, staying here might prove more hazardous to my health, and I don't mean just because of this bite wound. I thought that Herschel would've visited here by now, but he hasn't. Maybe Lucinda told him that I was here. Maybe Lucinda told him what we did together, once again. Either way, I suppose I do want to see Herschel, sooner rather than later before I succumb to this diseased condition.

I'm not sure how prepared I would be to have a serious conversation about my future with Lucinda or my fatherly responsibility for Celeste, if my initial reunion with Herschel came to that. I'm hopeful all of that can be put on the back burner for the time being until I'm better and Grammy's health care is resolved. I just can't imagine Grammy surviving much longer like this, especially if I'm no longer able to function myself.

Too bad Grammy never had a phone. I'd say I really would call for help at this point.

# MAY 4TH

## GRAMMY'S CABIN

The storm hit this afternoon. Its first surge raked the treetops with the most violent wind I can recall ever seeing. The lightning was everywhere with bolts exploding all around the cabin. I feared a tornado was imminent. Grammy wasn't at all concerned with the storm, though. She just hopped around the cabin by lantern light as though whatever transpired outdoors was completely irrelevant.

It seems odd to me that this violent of a storm should hit after what Herschel said to me when he visited yesterday. He remarked how unusually dry and warm the spring had been this year. Herschel seemed much more interested in the weather yesterday than anything else. Can't say I really blame him for his aloofness with regard to me, especially after he noticed the condition of my arm. He didn't offer to drive me to a doctor's office or anything. He just said that I should have my arm "looked at."

Herschel did remark that his heavy equipment operator work has been sporadic over the past couple of years. I didn't inquire further about that, but it did make me wonder if he mentioned that to suggest he wasn't in the best state financially right now. He might also have been implying that he hoped for some kind of compensation for the help he has provided Grammy over the years of her illness, which could be confounded by my sudden return here.

I had hoped that Grammy would apprise me of any financial arrangement she made with Herschel. Her only response to this question when I raised it was another scrawled handwritten message that I am her heir. I know that any arrangement she made with Herschel is ultimately none of my business, but it would help me to know how to deal with Herschel better going forward. That is, if we do indeed continue to interact with each other.

Anyway, at least Herschel's visit yesterday didn't lead to a fight or worse. Plus, I didn't suspect that anything was amiss between him and Lucinda by the way he acted. Or maybe Herschel just didn't feel compelled to involve me in his affairs at this time. He definitely is the reserved type, anyway. Still, the finality in his tone when we said goodbye after his visit seemed to ring the same as it did ten years ago when we last saw each other at the boarding gate for my flight in Cincinnati for London.

It truly saddens me that the past friendship between Herschel and me is now this void between us. We were much more like brothers than friends growing up together. I might be reading more into our first reunited meeting with each other than I should, but it sure seems to me like the distance between us can't be traversed. I hope I'm wrong about that.

# MAY 6TH

## GRAMMY'S CABIN

W hen I heard the mourning dove coo amidst the dense canopy in the distance, I set the shotgun against the well. I then painfully overlapped my hands, and with the knuckles of my thumbs for a reed, I blew a deep, dove-mimicking whistle into my cupped palms. I fluctuated the call as I waggled the fingers of my good hand, then repeated the dove call until I heard the squeak of the dove in flight approaching me.

The hunt was much more painful for me than the dove. It took me about an hour to loosen the rigidity that has afflicted the wrist and elbow of my bad hand. Even after I did regain some flexibility in my hand and arm, I had to move it gingerly. Any sudden movement with that arm shot pain through my neck and chest. I knew that even the measured recoil from the 20-gauge would be unbearable, and it was.

But when the dove landed on a barren branch within range for me to have a clean shot, I had to shoot. Had I been compelled by sport alone, or even food, I doubt that I would've sighted its little round pigeon eye, but I was driven by an appetite that I had not known before: I craved blood more than meat. The blood-thirst crazed me when I saw that the eight-shot load from the shotgun held to spray just the mourning dove's head.

Before I had even started to hunt for something that could slake my blood-thirst, my mouth was filled with a salivated paste that clung to my palate and tongue. I tried to swish water within my mouth so that I could spit the paste, but the water not only didn't dissolve the paste, it somehow seared my mouth and gums. Also, the paste blocked my ability to swallow to the extent that I constantly drooled an awful foam.

So, I was more than just pleasantly surprised when the natural juices of the raw meat, and the little bit of blood that I licked from the dove carcass, did, in fact, dissolve the paste within my mouth. The drooling stopped, too, at least for a while. Unfortunately, I was just temporarily relieved from my affliction, not cured of it.

When I awoke this morning from the sweetest and deepest sleep, the craving for more raw meat and blood cramped my stomach, and the hydrophobic paste had returned to my mouth. I suspect that I'm in the throes of a vicious cycle in which I have to hunt daily for the prey that can appease my rapacious appetite, just so that the paste in my mouth is diluted enough for me to swallow and breathe.

I hadn't shared my game with Grammy, though, and I worried about what she might do for food until I saw the delivery man coming. I didn't realize that she had an arrangement with a grocery store in the nearest town to deliver food to her cabin once a month. I hadn't asked Herschel about providing any food during his visit, and he didn't say anything about any deliveries here. Grammy never informed me of this delivery schedule either.

When the delivery man plodded along the path from the road to the cabin, he pulled a dolly that squeaked intermittently at its two wheels. I investigated the noise that I didn't recognize at first until I saw the delivery man. When I realized he was bringing food, my drool turned on like a faucet.

The patch sewn above his uniform shirt pocket indicated that this man was "Ed." Perhaps I greeted Ed too exuberantly, and once I wiped the drool from my face, Ed seemed anxious to deliver his load and leave. Of course, Ed might've been behind on his delivery schedule, for all that I know. And he might've had a natural stutter, but whatever his hurry, Ed averted my eyes and wasn't much interested in talking about the weather.

I do suspect that my appearance rather alarmed Ed. Maybe not only because I'm filthy and unkempt right now, but also because I just happened to be here. I doubt he had ever encountered someone along the path on his way to deliver groceries to Grammy. He might've been disturbed enough by Grammy's appearance to already be somewhat apprehensive about coming to the property.

Or perhaps he caught the sight and smell of the grotesque wound bulging from my arm. Whatever the case, Ed didn't talk in his rush to transfer the bags of ice and two boxes of groceries to the porch. He stammered his farewell before he jogged away with the dolly rattling behind him in his dash back to his vehicle. Ed didn't receive any payment for the delivery, so I'm assuming that Grammy had arranged to pay for it in advance.

Ed did cast once glance at me before he fled completely from my view. Shortly thereafter, I heard the muffled ignition of Ed's delivery transport. I suppose that I should've thanked Ed for the delivery, especially since the arrival of food here was such a welcome sight to me. Before I could pilfer through the boxes, I heard the thumps of Grammy hopping toward the porch. She seemed as delighted as I was about the food delivery.

Grammy came outside. I knew where she kept the ice and meat. Without any electricity for a refrigerator, Grammy had to keep whatever needed to be cool underground. She had a pit lined with rock that extended a few feet below ground, and this storage site was kept further cooled by its proximity to the well. The top of the pit was covered by a cast-iron lid of the cauldron she has on the property. It's heavy enough to resist the advances of raccoons and any other varmint that might seek to raid the wares stored there. I had taken the two bags of ice with my good hand, intending to go to the cooling pit, but Grammy croaked her summons for me to stop.

I set the ice back on the porch, then followed Grammy into the cabin. She had placed a large cooler there beside the pantry. I had noticed the cooler before, but when I opened it then, it was empty. Grammy motioned for me to bring the rest of the delivered groceries to her. I did just that, then I separated the perishables from the can goods so that Grammy could position the meat how she wanted within the cooler. She finished her task then sprang erect in her chair. I thought that something was wrong with her until she addressed me, croaking her message that she didn't use the cooling pit any longer because she often had groceries delivered to her cabin on a monthly basis.

I acknowledged her before I started to put the dry and canned goods into the pantry, but Grammy lurched for my forearm. At first, I thought she was going to bite me again. I instantly recoiled from her until it was clear to me that she wanted my attention. I waited for her to address me again as she groped along the floor below her chair. She had set aside a package of meat. I thought she was going to give the package to me so that I could prepare it for her.

Not so. I watched her bony fingers pry at the tape along the back of the package until she successfully removed the wrap. Instead of handing the package to me, Grammy pulled one of the strips of raw beef liver from those three or four within it. She dangled the strip in front of me.

She then told me to eat it. Its raw, bloody smell invoked the crazed thirst in me. I snatched the beef liver strip from Grammy and bit into it. As I devoured it, I noticed that Grammy had pulled another strip from the package. She then stuffed part of the strip into her toothless mouth and sucked upon the liver.

That's when it dawned upon me that Grammy was afflicted with the same blood-thirst as me. I felt thunderstruck. I then understood what I am now and the transition that I'm undergoing. As much as I'd like to attribute the symptoms to something else, I have to face the fact that, since she bit me, I've been undergoing a change unlike anything else I've ever experienced. I'm about to be altered, but I still find it hard to believe that I'm actually about to transform into a werewolf, although I would prefer to be a lycanthrope instead. That sounds better.

I'd really rather not believe I'm either, but I have to heed what I've witnessed and what's happened to me. There's just no explanation for what became of the wolf. As much as I hate to admit it, the wolf had to be Grammy. The idea that specimens of two unrelated mammalian families could somehow be transmuted into the same individual creature still seems like the preposterous residue of superstition and folklore. To actually believe that this lycanthropic transformation is possible strikes me as symptomatic of mental illness. Oh well.

I suppose if there is an ideal place to become a lycanthrope, this would be it. I asked Grammy about the nature and extent of my affliction. She just croaked away about how it was better to buy beef liver than chicken liver because blood was more readily drawn from the beef. I had to admit that the liver did slake my blood-thirst and suppressed the return of the paste to my mouth.

Even hours later, I feel nourished and comfortable, except for the wound to my arm, that is. I also asked Grammy about my arm, but she just waved me away. Since I've apparently decided to forego medical treatment and Grammy doesn't seem worried about the bite, I suppose that I'll just have to accept the consequences of whatever happens to me.

But the bite wound sure is ugly, probably even worse looking than it is painful because the feeling in my forearm is just about gone. I do get shots of pain up my arm to my shoulder now, though, but my wrist and hand do seem to work better than they did earlier. It looks like I'll live to keep writing all of this down.

Still, every time I look at my arm, I'm more and more concerned by its deterioration from the bite wound. The bulbous lump protruding from the meat of my forearm is completely black now and apparently rotten. The knot itself continues to swell and spread. There are red streaks that extend up my arm. Those streaks are darker and wider now, as are the blotches up and down my arm.

I suppose that the only aspect of my condition that actually has improved is the delirium: it's far less frequent than at first. However, when it does hit me, the episode is far more severe. The fever remains, but it seems to climb then drop without any real debilitating effect.

The cold sweat and hunger cramps that afflicted me after Grammys bite are gone, having been replaced by the blood-thirst and my compulsion to satiate it. At least I still retain the prolonged luxury of sleep without screaming myself awake. I continue to awake within the same dream night after night, but it's a different now than it was with the Nightmare Eagle. My dream body remains at rest in the same den on the ledge below the rock slab of bridge. After the brief awakening within my dream, I almost immediately return to sound sleep. That's all it is.

As much as I'd like to make some kind of plan for my future in terms of employment, living arrangement, transportation, and the like, I suppose that I'll have to content myself with biding my time here at Grammy's until the seemingly inevitable totally overtakes me and renders me with the legacy that Grammy had bequeathed to me through her bite.

## MAY 7TH

### GRAMMY'S CABIN

Another storm blew through here late last night. The fireworks came with it. The sky now is cloudless blue. The air today is quick and chilled. It was cool enough this morning for me to don a long-sleeved shirt. It was a good thing that I dressed this way because Lucinda and Celeste showed up here shortly thereafter. I wouldn't want either of them to be alarmed by the condition of my arm, which would undoubtedly horrify both of them.

Lucinda did ask to see my wound, though. She said that Herschel told her about it. Lucinda even brought a bottle of hydrogen peroxide for me. I took the bottle from her but declined her offer to apply the liquid to my arm. I knew that if I showed my wound to them, they would leave at once. I didn't want them to leave because I found myself captivated by the sight of Celeste, who has the beautiful eyes and blondish hair of her mother. She's somewhat too tall and gawky, but I'm sure that she'll flower in time to rival the loveliness of her mother.

Celeste does not resemble me any more than she bears any

likeness to Herschel. Perhaps Lucinda was busier those ten years ago than either Herschel or I can imagine. I'm not sure how to proceed with this biological claim that Lucinda has made. If Celeste really is my offspring, she might have to live her whole life without ever knowing that. I do doubt that Lucinda would deprive her of that information, and she may have very well already told Celeste about me.

I also wish that Lucinda hadn't told me something else. It was about the very last thing that I wanted to hear. First, she had to convince Celeste to wander over to the fringe of the woods so that she was out of earshot. She then told me that she thought she was pregnant. By the tearful look in her eyes, I didn't have to ask her who she thought the father was.

This certainly complicates matters beyond what they already were. If Herschel knows about this, I could be in store for real revenge. I doubt that Herschel would kill me at this point. He probably figures that I'm already doing a good enough job at that all by myself.

I really do feel like I'm halfway to rigor mortis now. The red streaks have extended along the whole bitten side of my body and spread to my chest. My torso is stiff, and my bad arm won't bend at all. At least my good hand isn't affected yet. I'm quite sure I'd be absolutely driven out of my mind for good if I couldn't write all of this down. I'm guessing it's just a matter of time before the infection and affliction debilitates my entire body, though.

At least the worst didn't happen in front of Lucinda and Celeste. I tried to seem at ease as best I could, but Celeste detected that something was wrong with my arm. When she asked me about it, I told her that I think I might've been bitten by a wolf and was turning into a werewolf. That amused Celeste, but Lucinda didn't think my reply was funny at all. She entreated me to drive me to the hospital for treatment before my condition deteriorated. I lied when I told Lucinda that I was feeling much better from the spider bite on my arm. I partly said that to help Celeste feel more at ease around me.

Lucinda tried one last time to convince me that medical treatment was in order. She even offered for me to spend the night at her house with her and Celeste. She said Herschel was gone to Lake Cumberland for the weekend. The surge that coursed through me from this disclosure tempted me. I paused in my reply to her offer in order to survey her in her ripe beauty. Her halter top seemed even tighter in its containment of the unsupported contour that it emphasized. Her short shorts absolutely gripped her in the showcase of her sumptuous lower body.

I almost acquiesced to her but stopped myself from indulging in her temptation. When I declined to go with her, she informed me that she and Celeste would visit me again tomorrow to make sure I was improving. I don't really want anyone around me in the event that I transform beyond my ability to control myself from total lunacy. I could, however, use some company besides Grammy, who infuriates me with her unwillingness to talk at length with me about my condition.

So, I suppose I would gladly receive Lucinda and Celeste tomorrow if they do show up here. Perhaps Lucinda will shed more light on her condition. I suspect that she already knows for sure that she really is pregnant. Otherwise, I don't know why she would mention it, unless, of course, she thought claiming to be pregnant with another one of my seeds might draw me closer to her. If she's after a commitment from me, she won't get it. I'm just unwilling to live with Lucinda or any other woman at this point.

I do hate to force an issue like this solely upon Lucinda, but she'll decide what she wants to do either way.

Lucinda and Celeste didn't stick around long enough to be here when Grammy finally woke up. That's probably just as well because she's likely to ignore them like she ignores me. No matter how hard I try to get Grammy to disclose more to me about my condition, she just grunts and waves me off. I really feel like I should know more about this affliction and whatever legacy is attached to it by virtue of Grammy basically bequeathing it to me the way that she did. I guess I can't really demand anything from Grammy, though.

Oh well. We'll see what tomorrow has in store.

That is provided, of course, tomorrow is there for me.

I just don't know.

# MAY 8TH

## GRAMMY'S CABIN

Today was Mother's Day, at least that's what Celeste told me this morning after she and Lucinda arrived here again. I suppose that our gathering qualified for a genuine Mother's Day meeting, despite the illegitimacy involved. Lucinda's presence here and Herschel's absence pretty much confirmed for me that those two definitely are pursuing their separate ways.

The prospect of Lucinda's pregnancy didn't surface today, though. I'll just bide my time with that. I suppose I'm willing to contribute to Lucinda's well-being if she is pregnant, but, right now, I can't afford to buy a bucket. I suppose that if we're both stranded and desperate here, we might as well be together with our children. I don't know. There just doesn't seem to be much else for me to do now.

Of course, sucking on beef liver might give Lucinda and Celeste some pause. They both might be hightailing through the woods back to Herschel's house if they saw me come feeding time.

At least I have Grammy. I'm content to linger here and care for her in whatever way she needs. She obviously wants to remain here until she dies. I have to remind myself at times that the only real reason I'm here at this point is to tend to Grammy's comfort. As ornery as Grammy is, she might last another twenty years. I'm pretty sure I'd be burned out on sucking blood from beef liver long before then, but then again, Grammy might have more beef liver in her future than I do. I'm not sure how much more I can take or how much longer I can make it.

Lucinda didn't seem to think that I looked too deteriorated. She didn't remark to me about my condition, anyway. I hope she has enough sense to start to exclude me from any of her plans. Yet, she did show up here today on Mother's Day of all days. That tells me she doesn't have many options that don't involve me. I find that hard to believe, given as physically gorgeous as she is. Maybe she really does want to be with me out of choice and not desperation.

Regardless of what happens to me and my illegitimate little family, I'm uplifted to know that Grammy can function just fine without me. She has blazed paths within her mind that lead her where she can't see. I've made a conscious effort to return anything that I use to the exact location where I found it so that Grammy can find it if she needs it based upon her memory.

Likewise, I don't let objects clutter on the grounds. I wouldn't want Grammy to stumble over something she doesn't realize is there. I had removed a branch that the storm had deposited upon the path between the cabin and the well just in time for Grammy to pass without incident. She was on her way to her tub. She decided to give herself a bath for Mother's Day, I suppose. Rainwater had filled the tub about halfway, and Grammy drew well water to fill the tub the rest of the way. She didn't remain within the tub all that long, but she hadn't finished by the time Lucinda and Celeste arrived here this morning. After she did finish her bath, Grammy hopped right toward the three of us, her gown fluttering behind her as she croaked her greeting to Lucinda and Celeste. She must've heard them when they met me.

Celeste had seen Grammy before at Herschel's house. She understood that Grammy suffered from horrible maladies and addressed Grammy with sweetly polite formality. Yesterday, though, probably was the first time that Celeste had seen Grammy at the cabin, unless she had come with Herschel to visit. Celeste didn't seem as gawkish today as she did yesterday. She also seemed a lot more interested in the cabin and its surroundings today. After Grammy excused herself and reentered the cabin, Celeste whispered in amazement to Lucinda that Grammy had bathed outdoors. It was understandable enough for Celeste to think that was strange, or maybe she just thought it was too cold outside or the water too dirty.

Celeste also showed interest in some of the things on the ground, like the well. She giggled wholeheartedly when she drew a bucket of water from the well. I then showed Celeste the pit beside the well where meat was kept during warmer months. She was intrigued by the idea that people without electricity had to preserve meat in a much different fashion than with the means of mechanical refrigeration.

Celeste was also interested in Grammy's smokehouse. I explained to her that this is where the fall slaughter of livestock was kept. We entered the smokehouse, and I pointed out the hooks that hung above us, telling her that meat would hang from the hooks in order to smoke it for preservation. I told her that Grammy had only used the smokehouse for pork, but that she had stopped raising pigs for slaughter many years ago. I intended to relate more about the smokehouse to

Celeste, but she crinkled her nose and said she wanted to leave.

She crinkled her nose even more when we reached the outhouse, but she then burst into laughter when she spotted the crescent carved from the outhouse door. I explained that the crescent was functional, as it angled essential moonlight into the outhouse for that nocturnal dash for relief. We didn't linger at the outhouse, though, or open the door to have a look and a smell inside.

The coal pile was our next stop on our tour of the grounds. The jagged lumps of coal seemed to fascinate Celeste as she handled some of them. She wanted to know how the coal was formed. I told her what I could remember about how the compressed fossilized material was created. I also shared with her what I knew about the uses of coal, including for a potbelly stove like the one inside of Grammy's cabin. That's when I suggested that we go inside of the cabin to have a look at the stove.

Just as Celeste and I entered the cabin, Grammy was about to heat some soup on the stove top. I explained to Celeste how the cooking part of the cast iron stove worked, and also how the smoke vented through the stovepipe that extended out of the cabin roof. She seemed to marvel at the stove, as though she had never seen one before. I'm somewhat surprised that she hadn't seen one of the stoves around these parts, but undoubtedly, the potbelly stove would seem like a whole different animal compared to a knob-activated range and oven like the one she knew at her house.

I'm glad Celeste and Lucinda visited today. Their company refreshed me. I just hope that I'm less hobbled when they visit again. My left leg is stiff at the knee, and it's painful to bend. Besides that, my torso has a diminished range of turn, and the streaks of my poisoned blood now course all across my stricken body. At this rate, I suspect that I'll be completely immobile before much longer. I again tried to ask Grammy about my condition and what would happen to me if I could no longer move. She just waved me off and croaked that she'd take care of me.

In turn, I'd like to help take care of her before I become incapacitated, if that's what indeed happens. There's probably not much need for me to fetch her any more coal. It's getting to warm to use the potbelly stove for heat. She has a propane stove on the porch that she's already used for cooking a couple of times since I arrived here. It has two burners, which is plenty for her. There's a propane canister already attached to the stove, so she's all set there.

Of course, Grammy doesn't cook the beef liver for herself or for me. Our taste for the raw meat and blood is one disturbing thing we have in common. I suppose I'll go back into the cabin now and wish her a happy Mother's Day.

# MAY 10TH

## THE SMOKEHOUSE

N

o clouds today. The moon is gone, too. I told Grammy I was about to drop dead. She told me to go to the smokehouse. Here I am by lantern light, but the mantle glow dims.

I can't feel my legs. Even my good hand is going bad now. Pain shoots up my elbow with each letter I write, but I must continue.

It's time for me to succumb to whatever this affliction is. Grammy still doesn't regard my condition with any sense of urgency. She seems so nonchalant about it that she gives me the impression that I'm reduced to this state out of some routine process, like she expected this to happen all along. Maybe she acts this way to reassure me that my fate is not the ugliest and most painful of ends. I'm prepared to believe there is hope for me. Somehow.

My mind hasn't left me yet, though. It still seems as sharp as fang against bone. I'm tired, but not sleepy. My thoughts won't shut off. Writing helps me keep track of them. At least this way

I can control their flow. The faster that I write, the more it sounds like the sentences are uttering themselves of their own accord.

The pauses in my thoughts are lags that I have to overcome in order to keep the rhythm going. I'm writing this now out of my fear that I'm losing consciousness again. The earth now wobbles and spins faster than the words can come.

But the nightmare is over.

I have no fear of sleep.

Just the fear of staying awake.

# DAYLIGHT

## GRAMMY'S PORCH

I t's taken a full day to regain the semblance of coherency.
I'm not sure which day it is, or even what month it is, but
the sun shines. The trees are green with leaves.

I had drifted in and out of consciousness during my transformation. Grammy visited me a few times that I can remember.
Each time she held raw beef liver to my mouth so I could suck
the blood from it.

When I revived yesterday, I could move a little despite the
soreness and spasms. I hobbled my way to the cabin after I
emerged from the smokehouse.

That's when I found Grammy dead in her bed.

Her blind eyes were glazed with peace, and her blue wisps
of lips crimped into the hint of a smile. She must've not died too
long ago. Rigor mortis hasn't set in yet.

I'm glad that her little, worn out body endured long enough
in this world for us to be reunited, despite these circumstances.
Her placid face now conceals the agony that must've stricken
her, and she does not seem to have died in anguish.

I need to notify the police about her death, but I'm still too weak to work my way through the woods or to the main road a few hundred yards from here. I'm shaky and starved. The streaks across my body have faded considerably, though. The knot where Grammy bit me now looks more bruised than gangrene. The paste has returned and is thick within my mouth, but I can drink water without too much discomfort now. Swallowing is coming much easier.

Grammy probably has a plot at the cemetery where her husband and two children were laid to rest. I'll have to check with her bank to see what arrangements she made. She most likely had a lawyer, but I really don't have any idea who that might be. She could've disclosed more information for me so that I could have better prepared for this eventuality. I definitely would feel a lot less anxious if I had some instructions by which to proceed. All that I can really do now is kiss her pale leathery forehead and squeeze her bony shoulders. I've already done my share of sobbing beside her corpse. I'm sure I'll do more before they take her away.

The moon seemed almost full last night. I'll see tonight whether it's on the wax or wane. As heir apparent to whatever legacy Grammy transmitted to me, I suppose I best heed what the moon conveys to me, if that does in fact bear some relevance to my affliction. I was more or less catatonic within the smokehouse, but don't recall much about the difference between night and day, moon or not.

However, one thing about the smokehouse does stick with me: I heard Herschel visit here while I cooked inside. Grammy was feeding a slab of beef liver to me when I heard Herschel's voice outside. Grammy hopped up so fast that the liver slid down my face to the dirt floor. She was out of the smokehouse in an instant with the door latched and chained behind her before I could assimilate what transpired outside.

I couldn't have moved if I wanted to do so, but I still could hear in my delirious state. I heard Herschel at the back of the cabin tell Grammy that he wanted to have paramedics come here with an ambulance to take me to the hospital. That's when I heard Grammy croak that I was all healed up, but that I had left anyway a couple of days ago to return to the Red River Gorge. I wanted to scream for Herschel to break down the smokehouse door and rescue me. I couldn't move or speak, though. All I could see was the slab of beef liver on the ground below my mouth and beyond the tip of my searching tongue.

That's all that I remember about the outside world during my transformation. The rest of my time in the smokehouse seemed like an overall lapse of consciousness with only glimpses of shadow and bursts of light. Now, it's a very weird feeling to wonder how long I was rendered incapacitated in the smokehouse.

The inside world is a different matter. While I didn't feel like I was consciously interacting with anyone outside of myself while in the smokehouse, I'm most definitely dreamt actively and vividly. The dream actually consoles me now and sticks with me while I'm awake. Not only does the dream portend of my recuperation, it has given my infected mind some point of reference for what sure seems to me like proof of the afterlife.

Right before I regained full consciousness, I emerged from the den below the rock slab of bridge. A crackle resonated above me. I wondered what made the noise. For the first time since the nightmare subsided into this same sleepy dream, I scaled the rocky slope above me to reach the bridge at the top of the cliff. There on the bridge was a giant nest much higher than me. I approached it on all fours, sniffed it, then took a look ahead.

Below the ridge on this other side was an expansive snow-covered hollow.

The crackle resonated above me from inside of the giant nest. I noticed that thick vines comprised the nest. I climbed them to reach the top of the nest then peered inside. There were three large eggs inside.

My first thought was that these eggs were those of the Nightmare Eagle, but that winged behemoth was nowhere in sight. That's when I remembered that my dream body had already killed that beast.

The crackle from the nest resounded again, only this time it prolonged as one of the eggshells fractured. I retreated before I could see what had hatched. I clambered down the vines of the nest to the rock slab of bridge, only to pause from further descent when a most familiar voice called to me from inside of the nest.

I climbed back up the nest to again peer inside of it, and there stood Grammy before the eyes of my dream body in the midst of eggshell fragments.

Grammy was covered in some kind of runny yolk, but it nevertheless was Grammy plain as day. I could smell it was her, then felt the surge of elation when I watched her hop upon her one foot to maintain her balance. When she patted her thigh for me to come to her, I scampered down to her. I whimpered below her as she patted my head. I licked the goo from her leg until I reached her varicose veins.

Grammy then lowered herself to my back. She wrapped her arms around my neck and croaked her instruction for me to climb the nest. I did climb with Grammy on my back, then I climbed down the vines of the nest to the rock slab of bridge. From there, Grammy dismounted my back, then she petted me as I sat on my haunches in front of her. She finally disengaged

and told me to go back to the den on the cliff ledge. I was reluctant to go, but Grammy ordered me to do so. I looked back at her
silhouette in front of the beaming light of the seemingly giant
moon behind her.

I whimpered for her when I reached the ledge below the
bridge. I waited for her to appear above me, but she never did. I
eventually curled up against the rocks and fell asleep again
within my dream. When I awoke from that dream, I found
myself fully conscious here within the smokehouse.

Now I'm here, and Grammy is dead.

Despite my harrowing and dreadful plight, I find joy and
benevolence in the streams of tears I shed. It is the spirit of
Grammy that compels me to feel this way. As much I feel like
she's cursed me with this affliction, I also find myself weirdly
grateful for whatever lunacy she has bequeathed to me.

Maybe now I can proceed into the world again, even though
I still have plenty of doubts and questions about who I really am
and what I've become. If the worst transpires, so be it. At least I
know that Grammy's flesh and blood courses through me.

I suppose I could really do for a bath before I set my course
for the real world. I probably should also shave this bushy beard
from my face. I'm not sure how to undo all of this corrosion in
my mouth, though. Maybe I'll gargle baking soda for a while.

Regardless, it's time for me to recover. I'll visit Herschel's
house tomorrow. I'll leave in the late morning hours. Hopefully,
Herschel will have left for work or elsewhere, and hopefully
Celeste will be at school. I really just want to see Lucinda now.
This surge of vigor coursing through me is something I'm sure
she'll appreciate. The mere thought of Lucinda and I pretzeled
together again is enough to make me gush right now.

But I have to keep my cool. I'll have to take care of whatever
needs to be done with regard to Grammy's body and the imme-

diate requirements after I report her death. I hope Lucinda can help me with that, too, but preferably after we re-introduce ourselves to each other in our most familiar way.

Who knows how the dynamic between Lucinda and me will develop? Perhaps we really are meant to be together. I can't promise her anything at this point, but I can share with her that I am open to the two of us being together if she and Herschel really are finished with each other.

What other alternative do I have, really?

## MAY 28TH

## TOWN DINER

I t was a good thing that I spruced up as much as I did, because I walked right into the middle of a Memorial Day parade today. Last night I used Grammy's washboard to wash my remaining pair of jeans and my only collared shirt. I also shaved myself with a straight razor that Grammy had in a kitchen drawer. It managed to produce a relatively decent shave despite not having the sharpest blade.

I had bid Grammy farewell before I commenced with my hike through the woods. I arrived at Herschel and Lucinda's house to find that no one was home. The cluster of homes below theirs appeared to be just as void of occupants. That's when I heard all of the commotion in the town below. As I approached, I realized a full-blown, small town parade was in progress.

The convoy of convertibles drove right past me on Main Street. The procession funneled into the gauntlet of the throng assembled along both sides of the street ahead. The occupants in the cars were young and old. One little girl in a woman's lap smiled and waved at me as the car in which she rode passed. I smiled and waved in return before I followed the exhaust of the entourage.

As I approached the crowd, a costumed man crossed the street toward me. I giggled at his attire; a coonskin cap upon his head and buckskin frontier outfit stuck to his overweight body, like he was a Daniel Boone well past his prime. He entered the doctor's office building where I unwittingly stood. I watched him through the glass front door. He made his way to the back of the room and entered another room, closing its door behind him.

I entered the building, too, curious to have a look inside. I stood in the lobby and took notice of the reception desk, the chairs for waiting patients, and the coffee table with magazines scattered upon them.

The Daniel Boone re-enactor then returned from the back room. He carried a doctor's bag and now sported a stethoscope around his neck. My presence startled him, but he soon recovered to ask me, "What can I do you for?"

I told him that my grandmother had died and that I needed the proper authorities to fetch her corpse for whatever legal procedures needed to be undertaken. I believe I rambled a little bit after that, about who Grammy was and the cabin grounds, but the doctor heeded the vital import of my blurted confusion. He said he knew Grammy well, then he motioned for me to walk with him from the building. As we maneuvered through the parade sidewalk pedestrians, he told me that he could sign the death certificate. I asked him if I should notify the police about Grammy's death. He then disclosed to me that he had treated Grammy several times and knew the director of the funeral home that Grammy had selected to handle her funeral arrangements. He said the director could transport Grammy from the property to the funeral home.

That's when we passed this diner where I now sit and write this. He told me to go inside here and wait for him to return. He told me he knew where to find the funeral director in all of the parade festivities. He actually has already done that, returning here to the diner to tell me that the funeral home director had arranged for Grammy's transport to the funeral home. The doctor had to leave after that piece of news, but he told me he'd be back to update me.

That was at least a couple of hours ago. In the meantime, I've managed to feast upon a cheeseburger platter, despite my inability to pay for it. The waitress, Julia, asked me what I wanted, and after I explained that my Grandmother had passed and that I was handling her funeral arrangements, she said she'd treat me to something to eat while I waited if I wanted. I lied when I told her that I forgot my wallet in my haste to come to town to take care of Grammy's transport.

Besides the meal, Julia has provided me with engaging spurts of conversation in between waiting on other customers. Her menu also includes quite the attractive physique with which to encourage me. She wears her jet-black hair in a bun, and her hazel eyes placate me for some reason. Her wonderfully creamy complexion appears true without any cosmetic illusion involved. Her eyebrows are wisps of black, and her face is seductively somewhere in between angular and round. Her nose seems petite, but not thin. Her lips are quite full and seemingly more succulent when she parts them to flash her straight, bright teeth.

As our intermittent conversation continued, she gathered the pieces about Grammy's death and my own situation, having returned here to my hometown after living for a decade in Western Europe and Rome.

As the diner crowd thinned out, our snatches of conversation grew more and more specific. I've also allowed myself the luxury to eyeball Julia more specifically, too. The blue uniform doesn't do her justice, but her white stockings do perfectly grip her long, thin calves. I've already let her black hair down in my mind, too. Plus, the corner of her mouth dimples from the crack of her half-formed smile.

I'm about to receive a refill.

Serendipity can dissolve the dark clouds of the sky within the mind during the span of a heartbeat.

Oh, here comes the doctor, I think. Hard to tell without the Daniel Boone gear, but I think it's him. I suppose I'm about to find out the details of Grammy's funeral arrangements.

# SUNDAY, MAY 29TH

## GRAMMY'S CABIN

They've taken her from here. The service and burial will be Friday. Evidently Grammy requested a service, even though she didn't bother to leave behind anything in the way of an attendance list. She requested a closed casket ceremony.

I watched them take the little old woman away, so I guess that's the last time I'll ever see her in this world. She was such a fragile and practically mutilated creature at the end, despite her sturdiest of natures. As much as I'll miss having the chance to spend more time with her, I know that she'll continue to live within me. That could be with reference to her bite and the disturbing legacy portended by that, but it most definitely means that our blood is one regardless of what happens next.

I notice my sense of smell is more acute now. I detect the lingering presence of Grammy on the property whenever I breathe deeply. I can imagine more vividly, too, as though a projection shows her chasing me around the grounds in a game of "Get Away." Her shadow shifts across my years, now. It is quite real and powerful in the darkness it defies by coming to light in its movement through my mind. I don't hear any voices or such to suggest that Grammy is haunting this place, but my memories of her buffet the leaves with a swirl of gust across the treetops. Her rest is at hand, it whispers. Her chores are done.

But my chores are just beginning. And, as it is, when work must be done, possession of an able and willing bodied partner is certainly a perk. My heart pumps serendipity enriched blood, now that I know Julia. I know that there's just no way that she can be from town. Complexity subsumes her character for me, mainly, I suppose, because she doesn't seem to belong here, but I learned more about her during our drive from the diner to Grammy's cabin.

I was pleasantly surprised when Julia volunteered to drive me to Grammy's cabin. I really wasn't fishing for a ride when I told her that I'd have to leave if I wanted to make the walk back to the cabin before dark. That's when she offered to give me a ride if I could wait until she finished at the diner.

During the drive back, the subject of college immediately came up. I mentioned how useful it would've been to study for a medical profession instead of literature, which is what I studied. That's when she told me that she had graduated with an anthropology degree from a state college. As weird as this might sound, I found myself physically aroused by that. Here was this attractive young woman in her mid-twenties working at a small-town diner with a degree in anthropology. Count me turned on.

I shared my own university experience with her in the hope that we might explore common ground, even though I didn't graduate from college. As much as I wanted to spend more time with her, I wasn't about to invite her back to the cabin to see Grammy's corpse and slurp some raw beef liver over a nice glass of well water. So, I had her drop me off at the road instead of driving onto the property itself. I explained the road to the cabin was more like a path and in rough shape at that due to recent storms. The ambulance didn't try to drive to the cabin either when the EMTs showed up to take Grammy away an hour or so after Julia left.

But as for Julia, that rough road explanation sufficed. She told me to drop by the diner the next afternoon I was in town. I told her I'd pay her back for the cheeseburger platter when I did make it back, but she told me not to worry about that at all. She added that she really enjoyed my company and wanted to see me again.

As much as that sounded like a cue for me to set something up more substantial between us right then and there, I just nodded and told her that sounded good to me, too. She kind of tilted her head toward me as she leaned forward in the driver's seat to meet my gaze. I crouched to peer through the open window of the passenger door. She smiled and winked at me, or at least it sure seemed like a wink to me.

I lightly tapped the top of her car, then I stepped back far enough so that Julia could still see me through the open window. She gave a little wave. I saluted her back, and off she went. I stepped back to the road so that I could watch her car travel down the road until it was no longer in my sight. I wanted her to know that I was watching her go. I just hoped that she was interested enough in me to glance into her rearview mirror.

I'd much prefer to get to know Julia better than I would jump into some kind of strained relationship with Lucinda, although Lucinda and I are a real match when it comes to tangling ourselves together in lustful passion. I just think that Julia and I might be a better match together. Plus, it would take us more time to find out if that is true or not since we don't have any shared history, unlike Lucinda and me.

I suppose, though, that I best tend to Grammy's affairs before I pursue Julia in this regard. Doesn't mean I can't visit her when I travel back to town. I know which bank Grammy used and plan to meet with them about any trust she might have prepared. Of course, she might've just had an attorney draw up a will. For all I know, it could be in a safety deposit box or filed in public records. Hopefully, her bank is in charge of handling her affairs in this regard.

Of course, the whole will thing could blow up in my face if she wills all of her worldly possessions to Herschel. Then again, Grammy did insist that I was her heir. As I sit here and absorb this place, I feel more and more at home, like I never really left here.

# MEMORIAL DAY

## GRAMMY'S CABIN

I suppose Grammy's revolver would fetch twenty dollars. I've sadly reached the bottom of the barrel where a mere twenty bucks is enough to provide a reprieve from looming despair. Or at least allow me to resupply my stock of raw beef liver.

It appears that I'm stuck with this deranged blood-thirst, but at least the festered mess on my firearm has receded to the point where it is just a discolored callus. Likewise, the streaks of infected blood are gone now.

Despite the signs of recovery, I'm still reluctant to return to town for fear of something happening to me that I can't control. But if I remain here for too long, I'll just be wrapping another layer of derangement around me because the one single thought in my mind now is this: I am a werewolf. The catatonia and oblivion within the smokehouse were the features of my transition. The haze and heat here now feel like they are smothering me with the doom of my changed identity. I awoke from my catatonia to the full moon beneath which Grammy died. Her lunar blood is mine now, and her blood-thirst is now my own signature.

I do wish that Grammy had shed a little more light on the blood-thirst other than how to satiate it with raw beef liver. I suspect that more—much more—will be required in the full moons ahead of me to slake that thirst in the future.

Despite this craving for blood, I really don't feel like I'm about to pounce upon some unassuming creature. It's the potential loss of volition that disturbs me most, especially if the pull of the moon does precipitate a transformation that renders me with the urgency to prowl.

I only have the example of Grammy to go by in this regard. If I'm prepared to believe that Grammy indeed transformed into the maimed wolf I saw, then I must recognize some of the attributes that Grammy displayed, mainly that she did have some measure of self-control while in shape shifted wolf form. Perhaps, that means I don't have to be a deranged psychopath biting and eating everyone in sight. We'll have to see.

The other aspect of this werewolf legacy that Grammy has bequeathed to me is that it is most definitely tied to mortality. Grammy's physical death proved that. Plus, she was able to live out her long, long life in her freedom despite the affliction. I'm assuming that Grammy was able to do this without feasting upon people, otherwise she most likely would have been apprehended at some point for the murder of those eaten. Again, that tells me that I do have some measure of control in this. I'm telling myself right now with the prayer that this will be reinforced later when I need the message to stick the most: I will not eat people.

There. I said it. I will not eat people.

I am a lycanthrope who will not eat people.

I have to believe that I really can restrain myself. There's enough damage wrought upon this planet without any contribution from me to desecrate it further.

The dream that I have inherited from Grammy conveys support for both the hope that I won't leave a heinous wake behind me and the certainty that I'm on the verge of a ghastly transformation. I don't exactly see my dream body, but I know that it is my perception that is engaged within the dream. I am a quadruped within that uncanny realm, and my perspective remains close to the ground. Despite the total darkness that engulfs me, my acuity within the dream exceeds my level of awareness during the daylight hours of normal consciousness.

Grammy, however, didn't reappear in the dream last night, but I did, once again, emerge from the den below the rock slab of bridge. The shell from which Grammy had hatched the night before remained strewn in fragments in the nest. I had climbed into the nest to see if some other sign of Grammy remained there but detected nothing. I shifted my attention to the two other eggs. I descended and sniffed them. These eggs didn't stir during the short time I remained beside them in my dream. My dream body is quite curious about what is inside of these eggs.

Finally, I climbed from the nest and scampered back to my den below the rock bridge. There, I returned to sleep within my dream. Before the sleep came, though, I again deliberated within my dream about what those eggs might contain and when, if ever, they would hatch.

I suppose only time will tell what will become of the remaining eggs, and me, for that matter. Tomorrow looks more unsettled for me than ever before in my thirty years. Of all the beliefs that I have embraced in the past, I find it somehow ironic that the only belief I can really embrace now is that I am a werewolf. I've already undergone enough transitional episodes to realize that some part of me seems to remain immutable.

Whatever that part of me truly is, I must do my part to make sure that it prevails regardless of the harrowing extent to which my life changes.

# TUESDAY, MAY 31ST

## THE DINER

I hiked through the woods at dawn so that I could reach town by the time the businesses here started to reopen their doors. First on my visit list was Grammy's bank and her executor. I can understand why the little old woman might've regarded me as the remnant of love in her life, but her generosity and affection for me have numbed me.

She alone has spared me from my penurious plight. Her savings account was a joint one with my name on it. Her will won't be read until later in June, but in the meantime, I'm as financially solvent as I've ever been. I have Grammy and her husband's railroad pension to thank for that. Twenty-thousand dollars to me right now might as well be a million. I can stand again without the vertigo from a penniless suffocation. I don't know what Grammy would've had in mind as far as how I would spend her money, but I'm not about to squander her savings.

I've already withdrawn seventy dollars. I chose this amount because that's all that I had when I landed in Kentucky. This seventy-dollar sum won't disappear as quickly as the other seventy did, but it probably won't buy me as much as the latter did. I have Virgil to thank for that. I'll have to pay a visit to Virgil as soon as I renew my driver's license and buy a car. I do cringe at the expense of a car, though. A decent one might make this sudden wealth of mine evaporate. Still, I've always wanted to own a car, and I really do need to have one now. I'd love to have that freedom to just turn a key and drive away.

For now, I'll just savor the seventy dollars. It's already five less than that now. I bought some breakfast here at the diner, even though it's lunchtime. It's been too long since I've had a breakfast of biscuits and sausage gravy. I can feel the grease licking at my heart like the tongue of a lost dog just reunited with its jubilant master. The glass of milk that I gulped down after I ate just coated my stomach with a silver lining. I was worried that the milk might unsettle my stomach, but so far, so good. The pot of coffee I'm drinking has already sent me to the restroom once and might again before Julia arrives for her shift.

I plan to generously compensate Julia for her kindness to me, yet I don't want to overwhelm her with too much too soon. Plus, I want to make sure she's interested in me and not my newfound wealth. I do want to see if Julia will attend Grammy's funeral on Friday morning. What a first date that would be. Maybe I need to ease into that one. I wouldn't want to blurt something to Julia that would make me wince later. This is not the time to bumble, but I'd like to celebrate. I just have to make sure that my enthusiasm doesn't get the best of me.

I know that Grammy wouldn't want me to mope about glumly. Still, she wouldn't want me to go off the deep end. It's just that this liberation is gaining momentum within me. I just can't believe how lucky I ended up in all of this. I hit the jackpot.

Then again, my benefit was at the expense of Grammys life. I'll pay my respects to her first by not doing anything stupid. Her funeral should sober me up from my giddiness. I'm surprised that she requested a funeral service since she evidently didn't leave a list of people to be notified about it. She also requested that her service include a eulogy that she prepared.

Julia just entered the diner. She averted my stare to reach behind the counter. Maybe the connection I thought we had was just delusional on my part. Or maybe not. She just motioned for me to approach the counter. It's time to find out what she wants.

# TUESDAY, MAY 31ST

## THE DINER (STILL)

I probably should just cash Grammy's savings account into travelers checks and return to my wife and life in Rome. Twenty grand might be enough of a reason to patch things up between us. It's not like I don't care for her or love her, but I just couldn't stand my life there any longer with the Nightmare Eagle constantly terrorizing me from sleep. Now that the nightmare is over, maybe I can return to Rome and resume a normal life, except for maybe this lycanthrope thing.

If I don't leave now, I suspect that I'll dip myself into something that will be irreversible. I ought to regard what I've abandoned before I like Julia any more than I already do. If I still really love my wife like I keep telling myself I do, I would just reappear at our apartment in Rome, and, at the very least, give ten thousand dollars' worth of travelers checks to her. I could then drop to my knees on our marble floor and beg forgiveness.

I can't imagine doing that, though. I don't want to be in Rome any longer, regardless of who might keep me company. Now, I might also destroy everyone who comes into contact with me because of this derangement that has resulted from Grammys bite.

I sincerely believe it is to our mutual benefit if I simply let my wife be to live out the rest of her life however she sees fit without me. We tried to be together for better or worse. It just wasn't meant to be. I'll probably wire money to her at some point to help her financially, but I'd only be fooling myself if I tried to convince myself that I might return to Rome someday.

Besides, Julia has invited me to her house tonight. She and some of her friends are gathering there to watch a professional basketball playoff game. I like basketball just fine, but I couldn't care any less about this game, its players, or the outcome. I only agreed to join the party so that I could have the opportunity to absorb Julia's presence without the shadow of the diner attached to her. I want to breathe her nocturnal aroma, even if that means wafts of party food and the scents of other guests provide a measure of olfactory competition.

Over the course of the past few days, I have to admit that Julia has managed to impress me enough to supplant the image of my wife in mind despite five years of marriage. The here and now is always loudest, but there's something alluring about Julia. Her reserved nature entices me to know more about her. I want the challenge of trying to make her meet me at a point where our minds could merge with our bodies in the most rapturous ways, if we ultimately do connect at such a profoundly passionate level.

I like the idea that this discovery awaits Julia and me. In less than an hour, we'll be getting that party started, I suppose. Her shift is over then, and we'll depart for her house. I'm in a back booth writing my brains out. When Julia asked what I was writing about, I promised her that I'm only writing good things about her. She smiled at me when she informed me that she likes to write in a journal, too.

Perhaps this journal is an ingress for us to share our thoughts together before we decide to advance the growing affection between us into something of a more lasting relationship. It seems like we have a shared interest in writing that, who knows, might extend to a shared appreciation of reading such classic literature as that penned by Edgar Allan Poe.

Wouldn't that work out nicely for me. I think I can still quote Poe on demand whenever the occasion arises, which, has not been very often over the past decade.

We're about to find out more about ourselves shortly because it looks like Julia actually might be getting off work a little earlier than she thought.

# WEDNESDAY, JUNE 1ST

## JULIA'S PORCH

I'd forgotten how comfortable it is to sleep a full night upon something other than the ground. Unfortunately, my back now feels like its hinged in pieces and my knees are stiff.

At least I can listen to music now. Julia's house has a screened-in back porch with speakers at each corner closest to the house. I found a radio station on the receiver inside that plays something other than country music. The broadcast of rock music resounds with static at times, but it's nevertheless sound for sore ears.

I sank into Julia's couch last night after her friends departed and Julia retired to her bedroom. I was aroused enough to follow Julia to her bedroom but wasn't invited. I'm glad that she established that. I'm not, however, someone who is bound to plead to appease what the body dictates. Still, I'm glad that her mind rules her actions and that she isn't desperate from the relative isolation here.

So, I slept soundly instead. The soft cushions usurped me. Julia's still asleep. She sipped her way through a few tumblers of

Scotch neat over the course of the evening, but she seemed quite unaltered by the proof from the bottle. Her friends were quite awkward toward me until alcohol loosened their tongues. It wasn't the lot that I expected here. There were two couples, from what I could gather, and I phrase it that way because I had to observe them for a while before I could surmise the relationships between the guests.

They were all quite cordial at first and grew increasingly louder as the night progressed. Although the basketball game wasn't the focal point that I imagined it would be for her guests, it most definitely was the main event for Julia. Her fervor toward the nuances of the game nearly alarmed me. She shouted at the images of players and referees. My only real interest in the game came when Julia blurted something. Fortunately, a couple of her guests were as disinterested in the game as me. They became quite disposed to converse with me as we sat together on the couch.

One of the guests is a dentist in town. He's from Knoxville, Tennessee. His southern drawl seemed pointedly crescendo to me, as though he spoke through a mouthful of molasses. For some reason, his speech conjured the memory of the mouth foam that I've experienced since Grammy bit me. The dentist's voice alone would continue to evoke peculiar sensations within me. At one point, he recounted how a patient of his had jabbered when given repeated doses of nitrous oxide before succumbing to unconsciousness and having his impacted wisdom teeth extracted. As the dentist related this to me, I experienced a burning surge throughout my throat and the sudden urge for a piece of raw beef liver.

I managed to quell this preoccupation by smoking a cigarette. It had been several years since I had smoked one, and the subsequent infusion of nicotine into my bloodstream buzzed me. I would smoke several more of the dentist's cigarettes until it seemed that my request for them peeved him. Once he had smoked the last of his pack, he announced that he was leaving. This was sometime after midnight. He left with his companion who had sat beside him on the couch.

The dentist and his friend both kissed Julia on the cheek before they left. The dentist's friend even placed his hand on Julia's shoulder before the dentist summoned him. I watched the dentist put his arm around the waist of his friend as the two men descended the steps of the front porch in their exit from Julia's house. I thought the two men were together, but they didn't overtly show their affection toward each other during the evening.

This seemed to confirm that they were indeed partners, which also shed further insight on the dentist's conversation during the game about his concern over an article in the local weekly newspaper. Apparently, this article detailed a case in a different part of Kentucky whereby a patient allegedly contracted HIV from a dentist during a dental procedure. His companion also seemed nervous when the dentist related the article to me. I can understand their concern.

In a small town like this in a relatively remote part of Kentucky, public opposition can amount to a well-timed shotgun blast. The dentist and his friend should be scared enough to exercise their freedom discreetly, even though they shouldn't have to do that. Hopefully, no undue attention will be drawn to them because of the article.

As for the other couple at Julia's last night, these two women in their twenties seemed to have a mutual problem with each other and their alcohol. They stayed until three in the morning, and the more they drank during their extended stay, the nastier they were toward each other.

Julia had to physically separate them at one point to stop the escalation of their antagonism toward each other. Nevertheless, they kept spewing vile remarks to the extent that Julia finally shouted for both of them to leave her house.

At that point, one of the women started to sob, and the other plopped to the couch and covered her face with her hands. I nodded at Julia when she glanced at me. I wanted her to know that I was there to help her if she needed me.

But Julia defused the situation by herself, convincing the couple to call a truce before they would leave on foot to walk the short distance back to their house.

I could tell Julie was exhausted after that, so I told her that I'd show myself out, too. She then offered her couch to me. I accepted with the condition that I make breakfast in the morning. She smiled at me then brought a blanket and pillow for me. She then retired to her bedroom.

# THURSDAY, JUNE 2ND

## JULIA'S

I never suspected that a shower could feel so good, but after a long time without one, the hot shower I took in Julia's guest bathroom before leaving for town this morning felt so great.

I also never suspected that a day spent in such a small town as my hometown could be so complex. The town itself isn't what's difficult to grasp, though. Many of the family owned businesses that I can recall are still in operation, including the clothier where I rented the tuxedo for my high school prom. I went to that same store today, only this time for a fitting to a different occasion—Grammy's funeral.

Grammy never did take me to town much when I was little and under her care. I never shopped much when I lived with my mother either. What little time I did spend in town was with Herschel more than anyone else. For some reason, I almost walked the mile or so to Herschel and Lucinda's house today. I can't understand why I virtually felt magnetized to pursue their direction today, but I resisted the pull to visit them unannounced. I suppose the fear of finding Lucinda alone again put an end to my deliberation. Too much potential drama there for me.

But I still very much lust Lucinda. After all, we do know each other so intimately, and we both thoroughly enjoyed ourselves together the two times we did give into our lust for each other. Perhaps part of me fears that I'll end up with Lucinda for more than just a tryst. I really hope that doesn't happen, and now, I'm finding myself more and more attracted to Julia in more ways than one. It also appears that Julia is attracted to me.

Julia came out to the back porch this morning in her satin night gown while I listened to music. She stared vacantly into her small backyard. I admired her calves and bare feet as she stepped to the screen door, then it struck me that her tall, thin build with high hips hoisted above her long legs reminded me of my wife again. I also noticed that Julia had a couple of mannerisms that were similar to those of my wife. She maneuvers through the kitchen much like my wife would, closing a cabinet door first by the side of the door before lowering her hand to the handle to shut the cabinet the rest of the way as quietly as possible. She also pours her coffee the way my wife does, by placing the cup on the kitchen table then bringing the coffee pot over to the table and pouring, then she returns the pot to its place.

I'd like to imagine that Julia resembles my wife in bed, too, with those long, thin legs and tussle of black hair in total orgasmic disarray at the height of intertwined passion. I hope to find that out, and soon.

Until then, I'll have to content myself with her company and conversation. That and my observations of her at different times and situations, like how she twirls her pen between her fingers before she asks her customers for their orders.

I suppose the overall drab appearance of her waitress uniform makes her seem even more refined and physically attractive when she doesn't wear it. My first impression of her still drew me in despite the uniform and the rather mundanely functional way she wore her hair. She's sleek in her own way regardless of how she dresses.

I also respect her for what she did after I ate lunch at the diner. I had shopped for my suit and shoes as well as some other items, including this new notebook. I felt refreshed enough by my outing and the meal to leave Julia a twenty-dollar tip, but she insisted that I keep the money. I wanted to pull her to me and kiss her lips, but I didn't. I just slid the twenty into her apron pocket, making sure she felt my fingers graze her. She smirked at me a little but kept the tip.

The tip was just a simple gesture to repay Julia for some of the kindness she has shown to me. It really should have been much more than twenty dollars, but I don't want to overwhelm her with disproportionate gifts. It'd be best for both of us if I don't succumb to the urge to be overly generous to her. I don't want her to think that I'm starting to objectify her, or worse yet, becoming obsessed with her. I don't want to subject her or me to that maddened state of mind that obsession brings with it. It is disturbing and potentially dangerous. I just want us to feel the connection between us and see if it will strengthen by virtue of our interaction together.

We both seem to mull our measured words before we speak to each other to the extent that the silence between us is filled with the true meaning of our dialogue. I like that breezeway that connects us. It's spacious, yet cozier than any foamy sentimentality or purely physical attraction could ever be. Besides, it contains the architecture that we'll have to situate around us before we can close in upon each other in a way that is becoming mutually more desirable with every movement we share in each other's company.

If Julia rejected me at this point, I'd drop numb, but I sense that all that we've done so far in regard to each other has been more of a survey to determine whether or not we can build an arch together over the breezeway between us. I believe we're headed in that direction, especially since she asked me if I'd like to return here to her house without her before her shift was over.

Julia even offered me the use of her car, but I declined. She doesn't know that I don't have a valid driver's license, but I did tell her that I wouldn't have vehicle or communication access if I returned to Grammy's cabin. Perhaps she took that information as a cue to invite me back to her house if she wanted to pursue what's started between us.

Whatever it is that compelled her to invite me to return without her present, I'm here. I strolled the mile or so it took to arrive here from the diner. She told me to make myself at home while she was gone, and I must admit that her home is a much more comfortable one than that which awaits me at Grammy's cabin. Plus, the intrigue of our connection and the fragrance of romance between us is starting to permeate the air here. We seem to be on the same wavelength.

However premature this affinity for her might actually be, I'm nonetheless relieved by its welcomed emergence. The turmoil from the lycanthropy that has consumed me now seems dissipated, almost like Julia has charmed me into a state of relaxation. I suppose all that remains for us is to commit to each other at all levels, but that will still require some work before we can fill our silence with even more meaning. I'm really not in any hurry to complete that task, but I do sense the urgency that I must initiate the process or else risk losing this first surge of attraction.

That doesn't necessarily involve sex just yet, which is merely what such a union between us would be right now. Julia and I need to establish a different type of intimacy first. I believe that this is what she wants even more than orgasmic bliss, although that might change if and when the time comes. We really have to reach a comfortable, ongoing expression of affection to which we can return during the time we are apart, so that we seek each other's presence as closely and completely as possible without actually being together. When she tells me for the first time that, "I've been thinking about you," I want that to be a powerful connection that can sustain our bond when we are apart.

I thought that I had established such a bond once before with my wife in Italy, but a nightmare intervened. Nevertheless, I know in my mind and heart that a man and woman must create this together if they are to resist the temptation to grow apart and ultimately embark upon separate ways. This is the vision that sustains me. It might be nothing more than an oasis in a loveless desert that tantalizes even more because it truly can never be reached.

But I have to try. I'll risk everything to venture toward that glimmer. If Julia and I can share this purest of drink in this desolate desert, our lives will be enhanced forever. Should we not find that drink together, then I suppose we'll have to move on elsewhere for different pursuits.

Again, I don't expect to make that determination anytime soon, or so I keep telling myself. I intuit that she's been wrung through some kind of wringer emotionally, and perhaps physically, too. I don't feel like I have to know about her tribulations because the details of her past aren't singularly relevant to what future she and I might share. My mind could change on that, but for now, I just want to get to know her better.

And if she gets to know me better, I wonder how she will react to the disclosure that I believe Celeste is my daughter. I'll eventually have to tell her about Celeste if the paternity issue becomes more pressing. Right now, though, I'm not going to mention Celeste to Julia or pursue matters about Celeste with Lucinda. If I should come to bear some responsibility for Celeste, then I suppose Julia will have to know, but who knows how long from now that will be?

Even if I wanted Celeste involved in my life, which I'm not sure I really do now, I have to wonder if my presence around her would cause her more harm than good, especially if I should, say, turn into a werewolf and eat her.

Now that I have some money, maybe I could just buy my way out of the whole Celeste issue. That probably would save everyone a whole lot of problems, especially Celeste. In the meantime, I'll steer clear of Herschel and his fractured family. I'll concentrate upon Julia and me instead. It seems clear that she and I are outsiders here.

# FRIDAY, JUNE 3RD

## JULIA'S PORCH

Grammy's funeral starts in less than two hours. The mid-afternoon start time allowed for Julia to come home from her breakfast shift at work before noon to get ready.

There won't be any funeral flowers unless someone other than me has paid for them to be there. This suit I'm wearing was an inane purchase. Grammy would've beaten me with a wet noodle if she knew I would waste her money for snazzy clothing on her posthumous behalf. Somewhere along the line, I'll have to justify the purchase, but I can't imagine how at this point.

I've never been to a funeral before, though. I just suppose that funerals call for men to wear suits. I mentioned that to Julia—the part about not attending any funerals before now. She seemed quite astonished by that. Maybe I just wasn't raised to have a breadth of warm feelings for those around me. I mean, I've known a few people who have died, but never felt compelled to attend their funerals.

But I am compelled to go to Grammy's funeral this afternoon. I never gave it a second thought once I found out that she had arranged for one. I can't imagine being any more grateful to someone who has lived than her. She virtually rescued me a couple of times in my life, this most recent time being the timeliest of all for me.

I just wish that she would reappear in my dream. She hasn't returned since she cracked through the egg in the Nightmare Eagle's nest. Now, I'm back to where I remain asleep within my dream. When I awaken, I only recall a few images and sensations within the dream den. Perhaps the dream is finished altogether. As long as the nightmare doesn't return, I'd be relieved by this conclusion, except for the urge to see Grammy again within my dream.

But I'll wait out Grammy and the dream on that score. My waking hours bring me too much reality to deal with than time to wonder about the realm of supernatural dream. I should enjoy my luxury to relax while the rest of Grammy's affairs are settled.

And that relaxation includes Julia. We aren't talking about matters of life and death, or anything else that would add too much weight to the silence between us. Last night, we talked idly for about an hour after she returned from work. Then she went to her bedroom without me, which is fine at this point. Despite the absence of any seemingly heartfelt conversation between us, she seems quite content to have me spend time here with her as well as the diner when she's working. She hasn't hinted at all that I should leave. In fact, it's been quite the contrary. She frequently asks me if I'm comfortable, what I'd like to watch on TV, what I'd like to eat, and those sorts of questions that couples ask each other when they truly want to be with the other person and want that person to enjoy the time spent with them.

Julia was quite amused when it dawned upon her that our first date is a funeral. She blurted that through an outburst of laughter, then she corrected her chuckle with an apology to me. I told her I wasn't offended by her remark in the slightest. I told her that I also found it odd that our first date was Grammy's funeral.

I still haven't shared much information with Julia about Grammy. I've mentioned Grammy only with reference to what I had to do in order to satisfy my obligations to the affairs that survive Grammy. Julia doesn't know about the money yet, but I did ask her if she would join me next week when I shop for a car. She seemed enthused by that prospect.

So, there's another date in the works, but I would imagine that there will be more added to our outing than just car shopping before we can consider that a second date. Actually, our second date might be something else. Julia mentioned that she would like to visit the place where Grammy lived. Up until today, I've only described aspects of the property itself, not the way Grammy lived, but today I did mention the cabin and the fact that Grammy had lived all of these years without the amenities of convenience that most of us take for granted. That seemed to pique her anthropological interest, I suppose, because after I disclosed some of the details about Grammy's lifestyle, Julia was even more vocal about paying the cabin property a visit.

No telling what might excite the anthropological side of Julia by visiting Grammy's property. Maybe that will be the key to turn her all the way on. It does seem to give me some traction because she seemed even more excited about that potential date than the car shopping.

But first dates first. We might very well be the only ones in attendance other than the funeral home staff, of course. She knows that I've bought a suit for the occasion. I wondered what she'll wear. She hasn't said anything to me about her wardrobe choice for Grammy's funeral, but I'm sure she has more selection among her clothes than I did.

And now my question is answered. Julia just popped out to the porch to inform me that she's ready whenever I am. She is wearing the most sensational black lace funeral dress I've ever seen. I'm no expert in funeral fashion, but her streamlined figure in that dress is enough to get a rise from the dead. Her proportions truly are seductive, with her full bosom and tapered waist. Plus, the lace, long-sleeves add a sleek length to her body that somehow sharpens the contour of her slender calves. I have half a mind to forego our funeral date so that we can peel the funeral garb from each other and see if we can't raise the dead right here in her house right now. But it looks like that will have to wait. Maybe tonight we'll try that.

# FRIDAY, JUNE 3RD

## JULIA'S LIVING ROOM

"Full moon siphons souls with beams of pull.
 The power of *The Spirit* shreds the flesh away.
 The Moon-Eyed dwellers in darkness have a friend
in the night.
 To protect them from the nightmare of daylight.
 Whosoever shall witness the arrival of this creature.
 Shall feast upon its freedom.
 Should its fangs sink into your heart,
 Rest assured all sorrow shall depart.
 Its glimmer in the distance embarks from its eyes.
 The wilderness entreats its will to survive.
 The light showers down with sparks that surprise.
 The fire of its soul glows forevermore."

The sheet of paper rattled in the preacher's hands as he
read the above to Julia and me. We were the only two at Grammy's funeral, and these words were read as her final request.
The preacher squarely looked at me after the reading and told
me that Grammy had written the words herself.

The preacher then aptly transformed the import of Grammy's passage into an affirmation of faith in his religion based upon the "power of *The Spirt*" part of her poem. He spun out a delivery that extolled Grammy's long life and intimate knowledge of the presence of the Holy Spirit in her life for its profound power to guide her through all the years she lived without ever losing her faith and love of life.

Of course, I know better. I could tell that the preacher added his commentary for himself, not for us. His voice shook when he read Grammy's message. It quavered even worse when he made his subsequent remarks. I thanked the preacher for his efforts. Undoubtedly, he must've fielded unusual funeral service requests in the past, but this one had to seem even stranger, given the import of the message and the fact that his audience consisted only of two people.

I sincerely appreciated the service. Without it, I would have never heard Grammy's poem. She certainly never read it to me when I grew up under her guidance. She definitely didn't mention anything about her words after I returned here from Rome.

And I needed to hear the message. Its meaning for me had to transcend whatever it meant to Julia and the preacher. I asked for the paper after the service. I had to read it again, both silently and aloud. I'll undoubtedly refer to it in the future for both clarification and inspiration. This message by Grammy clearly isn't just a poem: it is now my creed.

Julia delighted in the fact that Grammy bequeathed such a seemingly bizarre postmortem message. She asked me during the drive to the cemetery if Grammy had written anything else. I answered that I wasn't sure because I never even knew about this poem. Julia paused before she asked me why I thought Grammy had written her poem. I told her that it sounded like something Grammy would write, then I shared the part of my childhood about Grammy teaching me how to read and write from the works of Edgar Allan Poe.

Julia was wowed by this admission. She asked me in the car which story or poem was my favorite Poe work, to which I replied without hesitation, *William Wilson.* Julia drove silently after I told her this, so silent for so long that I finally looked at her as she drove. Her eyes were full and round when she told me that *William Wilson* also was her favorite of Poe's.

I never would've suspected that the mere mention of a Poe short story could have aphrodisiac powers, especially one as weird as *William Wilson,* but I sure got that vibe from Julia as she drove the rest of the way to the cemetery.

However, I wasn't about to share more about the true meaning of Grammy's poem itself.

That will have to wait, and perhaps will never be revealed to Julia.

As the funeral home staff of four pall bearers lowered Grammy into the ground in her casket, I couldn't help but sob. This was the real end of the line. Nothing more, forevermore. Julia squeezed my hand harder then and caressed my arm as she brought her face to my chest. I lowered my chin to the top of her head and sobbed again until the reaction passed. I wish I had spent more time with Grammy, not just at the end, but overall and over the years while I was gone. I could have at least contacted her more often while she was alive, but it's all over now.

Julia and I only talked for a short while after we returned to her house. She sensed my preoccupation and didn't seem to want to infringe upon its immediacy to me. I appreciate her discretion in this regard, even though my withdrawal into the void left by Grammy cost me the chance to enhance my intimacy with Julia. She retired to her bedroom for the evening after we ate a dish of spaghetti *aglio e olio* that I had cooked for us.

Julia and I haven't even kissed each other yet. Her consoling embrace at the cemetery is as close as we got. I might regret my preoccupation, but there's just no way I can spill my guts to Julia about all of this that's happening to me and how Grammy's poem directly addressed the transformation that I'm undergoing.

Plus, there's the fact that I really don't fully understand what's happening, not just the how and why of it, but what this werewolf thing actually *is*. All I know for sure is that Grammy bit me, and I started to undergo changes that subsumed my dreams and made me thirst the blood of beef liver. The poem tells me that Grammy knew all about my nightmare, and probably had one similar. The poem also portends of the unexpected in regard to the dream ahead of me despite the recent hiatus of the dream itself.

But perhaps most significantly of all, the *Moon-Eyed dwellers* mentioned tells me that my affliction is part of something much larger than myself. I remember that Grammy told me when I was younger that we were descendants of these Moon-Eyed people. She said they were here before the Cherokee Indians laid claim to this region. I hadn't thought about these Moon-Eyed people for a long, long time until Grammy resurrected them, so to speak, in her eulogy poem.

That doesn't mean I'm prepared to invest too much time or energy in trying to discern exactly how I fit into some kind of "Moon-Eyed People" scheme of things. At this juncture, suffice to say that I'm just another link in a legacy that'll unravel its manifestation before my eyes and probably within me by virtue of the physical changes that are taking place.

No doubt the vibe coming off of me about all of this was enough to send Julia headed for her bedroom without me. The cool thing about Julia, though, was that nothing seemed awkward about her just saying goodnight and leaving me to my thoughts. I appreciate that about her, but the more I find myself actually liking Julia for who she is, the more I do worry about harming her in more ways than one. I just can't stand for any injury to her, emotional or physical, because of my actions and choices.

That begs the question whether I should just leave now before we do get attached to each other. I'm sure she would resume her life just fine without me, and I'd be doing a good deed by sparing her the worst that can happen to her if, indeed, the worst is about to happen to me. This would all be altruistic enough, I suppose, but my problem with parting ways with Julia now is that I deny us both the chance to know each other better. That plus I really don't feel like I'm suffering from an affliction. I was far more afflicted before Grammy bit me by virtue of the Nightmare Eagle that kept me from sleep and drove me crazy in the process.

I'd go so far as to say that I feel more normal now than I have since I left for Europe a decade ago. I feel normal and at home, especially here with Julia. I'm not sure my body would heed the command of my mind if I really did decide to leave Julia based upon my fears of what might happen.

Now, if Julia bids me good riddance, that's a different matter. Undoubtedly, I'd try to change her mind, but I would ultimately abide by her decision. She doesn't appear inclined to part company, though. After all, I've not been the one asking to stay here at her house. She's asked me to spend the night every night I've stayed here.

I detect that Julia has gained her wisdom by trial and error, at least her demeanor suggests it. I doubt that I'm the first man who has more or less moved in with her. I'm probably not the first man to have lived with her here in this town, either. I know I'm jumping the gun a bit with this since we haven't actually moved in together, but it sure does feel like that's where we're headed, evidenced even more earlier today by her offer to launder my clothes.

That's another aspect of Julia that intrigues me. She's maintained her interest in me, even though her common sense must've raised question marks about my appearance, such as my lack of clothing changes and, undoubtedly, my funk. I've rejoiced in taking showers again, but it's hard to wear more or less the same clothes every day and still not disperse a rather gamy aroma, despite the recent showers and the washboard rinsing of my clothes at Grammy's.

So, our intimacy is going to have to be comprised of these small steps toward each other. I actually did take one large step toward her with my notebook in hand, but I thought the better of it. There's just no way she could digest what I would present to her. Not now, and maybe not ever.

Perhaps we can further fill the silence between us over the course of the next three days. Julia is officially on one of her vacations now, albeit not a very extended one. She told me that she hasn't had much time off for over a month due to staff shortages at the diner, and that she has pulled her share of double shifts to help the diner stay open. Apparently, a new hire and another employee returning from illness have cleared the way for her to take some time off now.

That means I'll get to see more of Julia, and by more of Julia, I do mean *more* of Julia. She treated me to a glimpse of her physique this afternoon after she returned from work. She changed into a pair of tight gym shorts and even tighter halter top without a bra before she changed into her funeral attire. She had me so worked up that the foam started to form in my mouth. I craved a slab of beef liver but was able to curb the blood-thirst with just oyster crackers.

If Julia crams herself into those shorts and wears that skintight top again, I won't even try to control myself. The only thing that prevented me from pursuing her body right then was Grammy's funeral. Perhaps Julia wanted me to physically approach her by wearing her suggestive attire, but I feared indulgence at that point could result in missing Grammy's funeral. Of course, she might've just wanted to be comfortable in something other than a waitress uniform or funeral dress for a brief time.

It did seem to me that I talked much faster to Julia after she changed into her shorts and top. Maybe she picked up that her presentation made me nervous and decided to change clothes sooner than she would've otherwise in order to dress for the funeral. We'll find out, just like we'll find out if I have some changing of the clothes of my own to do in the near future. I just hope that if I do have a beastly mutation in store that it pales in comparison to this werewolf movie that I'm half watching now while I write and Julia sleeps. This werewolf change in the film looks even more painful than natural childbirth or the passing of kidney stones.

Plus, this portrayal of the lycanthrope transformation renders a hideous and evil beast void of any capacity for the girth of human sensibilities. It's the worst of all that seems lupine. I certainly hope there's a gentler, more humane side to the creature I become, if that's what's going to happen.

One interesting aspect of this movie, though, that I really hadn't considered in relation to my own predicament, is the existence of a whole werewolf colony. Unfortunately, this movie also steers into scenes that are quite grisly with these packs of werewolves tearing limbs off screaming victims in viciously gory attacks upon the poor, helpless townspeople. The screaming from the TV has so overwhelmed the stretches of normal dialogue that I've turned the volume down to the point that I can no longer hear what the actors say. I don't want to wake Julia, either.

Of course, if I'm reduced to the state of one of these film version werewolves and attack like they do, I'll probably be waking Julia up one way or another. I just hope she's not rendered screaming from me attacking her. I just don't know yet if I'm destined to prowl with a rapacious appetite that knows no boundaries. Maybe I won't recognize people I know if I come across them after I transform. At least my encounter with Grammy as the wolf gives me some hope that restraint is possible.

Part of me hoped to view this werewolf movie in the context of research, but the forces that govern the mutations in this one seems just as arbitrary as any other werewolf movie that I can remember in relation to how the host spreads the affliction. I was also curious about the initial conversion process that occurred before the person actually transformed into a werewolf. This movie had an infection period that actually produced a dream corollary, which I did find interesting since I seem to have that element in my own transformation. But the dream in this film seems to be an extension of the perception of the person after the change happens without any vestige of the human entity remaining. I still feel human in my dream.

I also wanted to know how the werewolves are exterminated in the film until, that is, the primary method for killing these beasts involved the use of silver bullets. I'm going to guess that normal bullets would have the same impact upon me as silver ones would have, regardless of which physical form I'm in.

Perhaps there are other resources I can research. Julia has numerous anthropology books on her bookshelves. I've scanned the titles on the bindings and do recognize a couple of books by Carlos Castaneda that I had read in high school. If memory serves me right, those books did address a certain aspect of shapeshifting, but those transformations were accomplished through the use of hallucinogens, not human bite. Plus, I don't think those transformations in the Castaneda books produced werewolf creatures.

Some of the other titles about Native American folklore might shed some light upon my werewolf predicament. Then again, there are also some psychology books on the shelf. Perhaps I'd be better suited with texts about abnormal psychology than folklore books. Maybe the psych books detail the medical condition of lycanthropy itself: if not a shaman, then a shrink.

Or I can stick with Grammy's remedy. The beef liver really does seem to curb the blood-thirst craving. It worked for her well enough, so I'd be prepared to believe it will work for me as long as it did for her. I'll remain the optimist about all of this. I am, however, keeping a sharp lookout for the moon. I can't say that I've actively tracked what I'm experiencing in relation to the moon, but clearly Grammy mentions the full moon from the outset of her funeral poem. The cycle of the moon must have some impact upon the change. I noticed that the moon is now in its last quarter, so it will be awhile before, *"Full moon siphons souls with beams of pull."*

I guess I just don't have the lunar dipstick I need to gauge how the moon relates to my predicament yet. I suppose there will only be one way to find out. Until then, I best situate my contingencies as favorably for me as I can, which brings me back to the Gorge. I've been thinking about Julia and I taking a camping trip there. It's a much more inviting place once the inclement weather of spring has ushered in the pleasant conditions of early summer.

First and foremost, such a trip would allow Julia and me to connect together to a natural world that is awesome for its sheer size and beauty, including the various sandstone formations and other features that make the Gorge such a transcendental geological site. Some of the area might be more crowded now with campers, but I'm sure that Julia and I could find a suitable campsite of our own. If not, we could always opt to stay at the state park lodge or one of the rental cabins in the area. Regardless, this would give us the time and space to learn more about each other and create our own natural bridge between us through the great outdoors.

Secondly, revisiting the Gorge would provide me with some site location research. If the worst transpires and I find myself detected and hunted, I suspect that I'll need a lot more wilderness than what's available at Grammy's to hide. The Gorge and surrounding forest are ideal for a fugitive to disappear within without so much as a trace left behind.

Perhaps this is why my dream is transpiring the way that it does. It's showing me the place I need to find to conceal myself from others who might try to kill me, like these werewolves in the movie that's just finished.

In the end, lack of control and indiscretion killed them all, not just the silver bullets.

# TUESDAY, JUNE 7TH

## JULIA'S

This past weekend was a forerunner for a summer that is ripe to burst at the seams of everything here and scorch it all. The first surge of truly humid boil absolutely smothered the region. As much as this heat and humidity infuses me with a vitality that simmers the marrow of my bones, it also is aggravating when there's no relief from the salty sweat that stings the eyes.

Julia and I opted not to camp at the Gorge. We decided to attend a houseboat weekend party by invitation of her dentist friend. Actually, Julia was the only one of us invited. I overheard their conversation Saturday morning when he called to invite her. I noticed that Julia never did say that "we" would be going nor did she mention my name, but when she disconnected the call, she immediately asked if I wanted to go to the houseboat party at a nearby lake.

I didn't ask Julia anything about this on the drive to the lake, but once we reached our destination, the dentist seemed surprised by my presence to the point that he noticeably grimaced. He nevertheless guided both of us to the huge luxury cruiser houseboat that was docked at the marina slip. As we boarded the huge houseboat, rolling thunder rumbled and the swiftly approaching thunderstorm darkened the sky with its imminent rupture around us.

It felt like we had stepped into a cave when we entered the spacious interior of the houseboat. The air conditioning had virtually refrigerated the whole room, which was packed with about twenty party guests. Despite all of us in there, our collective body heat proved to be no match for the frigid air conditioning. Soon enough, though, the cabin cold was the farthest thing from my mind.

When the storm hit, and I do mean hit, people gasped at the violence that dropped upon us. Chunks of hail battered the boat, crackling everywhere louder and louder as the high winds buffeted the boat with such force that I wondered if we would stay moored at the dock slip. The lightning then detonated all around us. I peered pointlessly through the panoramic window, trying to glimpse a tornado or waterspout within the swirling rain shield, but visibility was nil. So, I did what all of the other guests did, which was to brace against something or somebody and hold on for dear life. I took the liberty to hold onto Julia, who squeezed me in return.

During that embrace between Julia and me, I glimpsed the countenance of disapproval upon the dentist as he clung to a seat and leered at me. That's when I realized that the dentist definitely wanted Julia to be there with him, but I'm still unsure why he would want that. Perhaps he wanted Julia to himself just for friendship. Of course, then again, the dentist might distinguish his attraction on some basis other than gender. His male companion at Julia's house during the basketball game wasn't among the guests inside of the houseboat.

I could only speculate about that because I didn't pursue the matter with Julia at the time and certainly didn't ask her dentist friend about it, but it dawned upon me that he might have had an ulterior motive for inviting Julia: to make it seem like he and Julia were more than friends. He might have wanted to project normalcy to his guests for some reason, like preserving his privacy about his sexual preference.

Perhaps this was an arrangement that she had agreed to before, only this time there didn't seem to be any kind of agreement in place. There is also the possibility that Julia and her dentist friend were more than friends at some point. I have to at least acknowledge this possibility for a couple of reasons, namely that I might have a rival I didn't know existed and, also, that Julia could have been intimate with a man who is sexually active with other men.

Whatever the case, his aversion to my presence there came across crystal clear. As soon as the squall subsided, the dentist demonstrated that he would pursue an agenda different from whatever he had planned for himself and Julia together.

The storm-shaken guests collected themselves and shortly thereafter resumed their activities, which seemed to be focused around conversing in cliques and partaking of the libations provided in the form of quite an extensive liquor selection. As for Julia's dentist friend, he imbibed upon a fifth of bourbon, guzzling directly from it as he mingled with the crowd. When it became apparent that the dentist wasn't going to address us anytime soon, I asked Julia if she wanted something to drink. Julia pointed at one of the pitchers of sangrias on the bar. I brought the pitcher and a couple of plastic cups back to our corner of the cabin. We sipped away as the cabin guests grew collectively more boisterous. We drank nearly half of the pitcher before the captain announced that the boat was about to launch.

During the boat ride, Julia briefed me about the nature of the houseboat gathering. The boat captain was a sales manager for a dental equipment manufacturer that periodically rented this type of deluxe houseboat for outings to entertain the company's select customers throughout Kentucky. On this particular trip, most of the guests were dentists and dental hygienists who had attended a recently ended dental convention in Lexington.

As the boat ride continued, the collective volume of the assembled guests reached the level of uproar. Only when the boat slowed to a stop did the crowd finally hush somewhat. That's when the captain announced that we had reached our destination, which was a cove flanked by submerged timber along the shoreline. The anchors dropped, and the guests resumed their chatter.

But when our captain wheeled out a cylinder of nitrous oxide from behind the bar, the crowd oohed and aahed. A hose was attached to the regulator of the tank, and a mask dangled from the other end of the hose. The captain then announced that he hadn't spared any expense for the entertainment of his guests, to which the assembly collectively cackled.

Julia's dentist friend insisted that he be the first to inhale the gas. He passed his nearly emptied bourbon bottle to a guest beside him, then he fitted the mask over his mouth. The captain opened the valve until the dentist motioned for him to close it. The dentist then knelt to the plush carpet and removed the mask. He had a fit of hysterical laughter before he collapsed to the floor with the captain easing his fall to the carpet.

The dentist soon revived from his induced lapse of consciousness. Others followed the lead of Julia's dentist friend in inhaling the nitrous oxide, but most guests didn't partake of the gas. Julia and I both passed on the offer, but we laughed along with the rest of the crowd every time one of the gassed participants dropped from their knees to the soft floor.

The captain sure seemed to enjoy his duties, as well. Every time he administered the gas, he yelled, *"There she blows!"* Once all the guests who wanted the gas had inhaled their fill, the captain wheeled the tank back to the compartment behind the bar. Julia's dentist friend had fitted the mask over his mouth three different times. He had also finished his fifth of bourbon in between his nitrous sessions.

Julia's dentist friend was by far the loudest guest on the houseboat. His inebriated howls filled the cabin when the captain announced the next round of entertainment. The hooting of Julia's dentist friend even surpassed the booming musical intro of the shockingly top-heavy, bikini-clad stripper who then entered the cabin from the concealed back of the boat. Several men in the crowd were treated to the undulations of the stripper as she successively straddled their laps and pinned their shoulders to their chairs while she smothered their faces with the massive breasts that spilled from her scant bikini top. She briefly lap danced with four of the men before she decided to dispense with the bikini top.

I would only see the stripper's enormity within the bikini itself because Julia covered my eyes just before the stripper discarded her bikini top. I didn't try to pry Julia's hand from my eyes, though. Instead, I took the liberty to graze the side of her hand with the tip of my tongue.

Julia didn't withdraw her hand from my eyes until the fiasco started. Julia's drunk dentist friend had toppled the top-heavy stripper. As he pinned the woman to the floor and mouthed for one of her nipples, the captain and two of his guests pulled their colleague from the laughing stripper. Julia's dentist friend shrieked his obscene desires as the woman's liberators carried her assailant from the cabin. The bare-breasted stripper then stepped to the bar and remained there until the captain returned to the cabin.

The woman's show wasn't only a striptease, though. Her work had just begun at that point. I overheard the fee for a half hour of privacy with the woman in one of the staterooms at the back of the boat. I was surprised that any of the guests were willing to pay the four hundred dollars, but two men immediately accompanied her in their threesome exit from the party room.

Apparently, there was at least one more stateroom at the back of the huge houseboat. I heard two couples strike a deal with the captain for their foursome to use another stateroom at the same time together.

I had only been to the dentist once in ten years while in Europe. I doubt the behavior that I witnessed on the houseboat is indicative of the dental profession on the whole, but it hardly prompts me to seek dental care anytime soon.

Julia and I decided to exit the party room and climb the outside staircase to the sun deck. That's when we discovered Julia's dentist friend with his backside stuffed into a large open cooler. He had been strapped to the empty cooler with bungee cords. Her dentist friend was unconscious as we stood above him. We weren't about to undo the straps that bound him. He clearly had found his place of repose for the evening.

As the night progressed and the party drew to its conclusion, a charter boat arrived and rafted up with the houseboat. The captain announced that guests who wanted to return to the marina should board the charter boat, but guests who wanted to stay on the anchored houseboat could sleep on cots and sleeping bags that were placed on the sun deck. About half of the guests left with the charter boat, but Julia and I decided to remain on the houseboat with the rest, including Julia's passed out dentist friend. I found a rolled sleeping bag that was actually for two people. Julia grabbed it and said we'd be spending the night together in it.

Before we retired to our sleeping bag, we talked about all kinds of lighthearted conversational topics, like favorite colors and animals, music and art, history, and other interesting items. The more casual our conversation became, the more affectionate I felt toward Julia. She was opening up to me in a way I hadn't seen before, and it warmed my heart.

Finally, the chilled night and our waning drunkenness compelled us to climb into our sleeping bag for two, fully clothed. The cold air kept us from sweating, despite our closeness. Julia fell asleep shortly thereafter, but I watched the stars of the cloudless sky above me as her sweet sangria breath fanned across my cheeks. I loved our embrace so much that I felt tears forming, but I, too, finally fell into the sweetest sleep.

I remained asleep and slept within my dream, too, until the maniacal cry of a loon jolted me awake. The purple incipience of dawn and the fog floating just above the glassy lake soothed me with its picturesque serenity. Julia recoiled at first when she stirred from sleep, but she oriented herself quickly then draped her arm across my nape and pulled me to her.

Our lips smacked for the first time, then she slid her tongue into my mouth. I instantly embraced her tongue with mine. That sloppy, tongue-sucking kiss lasted for quite some time with both of us softly moaning into each other's mouth for most of the kiss. We've yet to repeat that kiss. Neither one of us seems to want to rush into the passion part of our attraction if we can't savor each other's company first. Then maybe our affection for each other can saturate us with the deluge of ardor.

The morning swiftly illuminated what the darkness obscured. The lake is a beautiful place. I'd like to return to it someday under different circumstances. Once the dental contingent assembled *en masse*, the captain delivered us from the cove.

Despite the intimacy just shared with Julia, I found my mind drifting to the Girl from Ohio and her violet eyes during the boat rode back to the marina. For some reason, that memory of my exposed self in her presence at the Gorge kept recurring to me. The very thought of the Girl from Ohio stimulates me almost instantly. I just can't suppress the memory of her at the river when she saw me nude and I saw her in her bikini. She aroused a powerful urge in me from first sight. There was something so primitive in the attraction between us that I can hardly contain myself.

But I know that I'll have to contain my desire for her, or at least channel it into a healthier intimacy like that which I seem to be developing with Julia. I know that Julia has connected with me at a depth so different and more layered than I ever could hope to realize with the Girl from Ohio.

I quickly reminded myself of that on the houseboat as I casted my glance at Julia and she smiled at me in return. Julia and I really do seem to be involved in some kind of courtship ritual, and I find that refreshing. When the time comes for us to consummate our slow dance with each other, it's going to get loud and messy.

During the boat ride back to the marina, Julia's dentist friend stirred from his bondage within the large, empty cooler. He yelled for someone to free him. Julia and I shifted from his line of vision, but another passenger came to the dentist's rescue. We watched the dentist then crawl to the side of the sun deck, hang his head over the side, and puke to the level below. When he finished his vomiting, he curled into a fetal position and lay motionless on the deck as the houseboat motored ahead. I looked at Julia, who didn't seem the slightest bit concerned by the condition of the dentist.

The dentist remained in his fetal position the entire boat ride back, but when we did reach the marina, he stirred and repeatedly barked Julia's name until she went to him. He moaned pitifully while Julia helped him to stand, then he clung to her to keep his balance. He finally released Julia once the boat reached the dock.

As the other guests began to climb down the stairs from the sun deck, I approached Julia and the dentist. He refused to budge from his stance. Julia asked me to help him walk. I allowed him to drape his arm over my shoulder as he draped his other arm over Julia's shoulder.

I descended the staircase first then helped guide the dentist's feet to the individual steps during his descent. Julia followed him down, then we helped him off the boat and guided him to the dock. Julia scowled when she advised me that we would have to drive the dentist to his car.

Turns out that the dentist's car was a couple of hours away. He had parked at a farmhouse owned by a friend of his who was holding a field party with a pig roast and bonfire. During the drive, the dentist had recovered enough to inform me that the pig roast party was an annual event with bands and vendors. It was a crazy huge event, he said.

When we arrived at the site, his description was indeed the case. Despite the early afternoon hour, the field beside the farm-house was filled with at least a hundred cars already. We were stopped by a security guard at the property entrance, but when the guard recognized the dentist, he told us to bypass the field and drive directly to the farmhouse.

The dentist told Julia to park next his car, then he exited hers. He thanked her and waved goodbye to her, but he did not even acknowledge me in his farewell. During the two-hour drive back to her house, we listened to soothing music without vocals at a high volume. Neither of us talked much during the drive back until we reached the outskirts of town, then I turned down the volume and told her that I just wanted to thank her for taking me with her.

Julia thanked me for going with her, then told me that she really enjoyed my company. She blushed when I told her I couldn't think of anyone with whom I'd rather spend the time. Once we reached the driveway and she parked the car, she turned to me before I removed my seatbelt. She told me there was no one else she'd rather spend time with than me, either. She then leaned to me and kissed my lips. She kept her face in front of mine, then she told me that she really appreciated my patience with her in regard to the potential consummation of our relationship together in bed. I told her that the wait would make our arrival together all that much deeper and thrilling.

That's when she told me that I'd have to wait just a little longer, if I didn't mind. I tried not to pause too long before I replied that I didn't mind waiting more.

And I'm still waiting, but in the interim, I told Julia that my driver's license had expired while I lived in Rome. She drove me to the county seat yesterday so I could retake the driver's license test. She said that I could list her address as my residence, if I wanted, since it might be too cumbersome to use Grammy's. It nearly didn't matter what residence I used because I barely passed the written part of the exam. The driving part of the test was no problem for me, but the written part asked a few questions that I had no earthly idea what the answers could be.

Following the issuance of my new driver's license, we drove to a used car lot. The impulse purchase of a ride tempted me, but I exercised restraint. Not sure if I would've been able to hold out too much longer, though, if Julia hadn't asked me if we could go home. She said she was cramping and wanted to return home for some relief.

That was yesterday, and today is today. I've enjoyed getting my bearings straight by writing all of this down. It's bound to be more helpful to me in the long run. Now, I await Julia's return from work. She's back to the diner grind, but she'll have Friday and Saturday free. She doesn't have anything planned for those two days, as far as I know. After our adventure this past weekend, maybe I should be the one to make our recreational arrangements this time around. I, of course, would want for us to visit the Gorge.

I feel like last weekend instilled a certain fervor within both of us to be together somewhere other than this town, preferably where we don't know anyone else. It seems like it's going to get harder to just kick back and relax now. We have grown closer, and we're bound to put our feelings to the test of the most direct form of communication soon enough. As much as I'd love to spend the summer in Julia's air-conditioned bedroom making love to her whenever she's able to do so, that's just not going to happen.

Besides, I'm getting the urge to travel again. I've been "home" for too long now. It's about time to leave again. I fray at the edges whenever I have to sit in the same place for too long. I'm not sure what this compulsion to travel will entail, but I'd kind of like to go to a beach somewhere and breathe some dead-of-summer maritime air. As much as I'd love for Julia to join me on such a journey, I fear that she'll decline my invitation because of her job. She doesn't seem inclined to quit her job. She hasn't said anything to me that would indicate that she's pursuing more financially rewarding employment. That seems strange to me, but I guess she prefers for that part of her life to remain as simple as possible.

Hopefully, though, she can arrange for at least a week off of work. If she can't do that, I'm afraid that I just might have to embark upon my travels without her. I suppose that I'd be willing to wait for a month or so, if my affliction allows for it. This might be the turning point for us because if she can't arrange for an extended vacation from her job, then that tells me that she can't take the next step with me toward a relationship with much more substance to it.

First things first, I need a car before I plot any itinerary. I'm not about to ask Julia if we can use her car for such a purpose. I wouldn't want to drive a four-banger with nearly two hundred thousand miles on it for a long distance anyway. Besides being unwise, such a request would seem like a thoughtlessly disrespectful intrusion. Her car is her freedom, even though she could walk to work or ride a bike the short distance if she had to do without a car. If she ever decided to just clear out of this town, she needs her car to do so as quickly as possible.

Even though I've always managed to live without a car of my own, I've always had either metropolitan transportation available or the Western European rail system to get me wherever I needed to be. But it's so remote here in this part of Kentucky, I don't believe that I could maintain sanity over time if I didn't have the means to traverse the miles to somewhere else as quickly as possible.

No, I think it's high time that I owned a car. I don't want to get carried away with speed, but it would be nice to have something with some highway power to get up and go. I'd say a six-cylinder mid-sized car with low miles would suffice for my purposes. It's not like I'm bootlegging moonshine or anything, but I would like to be able to drive fast if needed in the event my affliction puts me in a predicament whereby detection of me in my transformed state jeopardies my freedom. If I have to play "Get Away" for real, I want to be able to get the hell away right quick.

I'll also need car insurance. Not sure exactly what I will need, but there's an insurance agency just a few buildings down from the diner. I'll probably drive in with Julia tomorrow when she goes to work. I suppose I'll stop in then and see what I need to do next to line up activation of the insurance with my car purchase.

While I'm in town, I'd also like to find out exactly when the executor has scheduled the reading of Grammy's will. It was supposed to be sometime this month, but it sounded like the date would be more toward the end of June. I'd sure like to find out what other surprises that glorious little old woman might have in store for me.

At least I think I'd like to find out what else Grammy might have in store for me. Hopefully, there isn't any more afflictions, though. I believe the one that is about to overwhelm me is more than enough for me.

# WEDNESDAY, JUNE 8TH

## JULIA'S

I knew it was bound to happen sooner or later. I ran into Herschel today in town at the insurance office. Oddly, I didn't dread the encounter, but I had to wonder where he and I stood, not that we really have anything to do with each other at this point. We actually talked quite casually while we waited for the insurance agent to spare some of her precious time for us.

I wasn't exactly surprised to hear him say that he wondered what happened to me after Grammy died. He then added that he didn't learn of Grammy's death until after her funeral. I told him the truth about what I'd been doing since Grammy's death. There wasn't any need for me to lie about that. Nothing had happened since her death that might reveal my affliction to Herschel.

There was, however, a reason for me to lie when Herschel said that he had visited Grammy with the intention of notifying medical authorities about my physical condition that had resulted from Grammy's bite. I wasn't about to tell him that I was in a catatonic trance in the smokehouse while he was on the property talking with Grammy. I had to lie that I went to the Gorge for a while after suffering my wound.

Herschel glanced right off of that comment to ask about my recovery from the wound. I lied again when I told him that I sweated all of the infection out during my prolonged stay at the Gorge, only to return to town once I had fully recovered. Herschel just nodded in reply.

The insurance agent interrupted the subsequent silence between Herschel and me. She escorted her serviced client to the door and ushered him through the exit while she assured him that his premiums wouldn't increase. I offered for Herschel to see the agent next, but he insisted that I go instead, which I did.

Perhaps it rattled Herschel to see me there unexpectedly. Maybe he thought I had left for good or had actually died from my wound. At any rate, after I found out what I needed to know from the agent, I asked Herschel to join me for lunch at the diner once he concluded his business at the insurance office. He said he would, and he indeed did meet me for lunch at the diner.

When I introduced him to Julia, Herschel seemed to shudder. Julia didn't seem at all bothered by the introduction, though, then she said that she already knew Herschel. She even asked him how he had been. Herschel stammered in reply. It was an awkward moment for him, and I can only imagine why.

Herschel blurted to Julia that he'd like a burger with fries and a Coke.

I capitalized upon Herschel's obvious discomfort, however, to inquire about Lucinda and Celeste. All that I really wanted to know was whether Lucinda was pregnant or not. He didn't say that she was, so perhaps I am in the clear on that count.

Furthermore, Herschel didn't say anything about a pending divorce between him and Lucinda either.

I had then asked Herschel about his work. He informed me that he was off for a few weeks. He asked me about my employment status. I admitted to him that I was in between work and reliant upon the savings account funds that Grammy had left for me in my name.

Herschel didn't seem bothered by the fact that Grammy had given that money to me. He didn't ask when her will would be read, either. I took the opportunity to thank him for all that he had done for Grammy. I extended my hand toward him for him to shake, which he did.

Soon enough, Julia brought our burgers to us. We ate in silence. After we finished our lunch, Herschel started to reminiscence about some of the times that we shared together. I was glad to hear him conjure those experiences. It was a refreshing change from the tension that seemed to have tightened itself between us. Our conversation lasted a while. It purged much of what seemed clotted between us.

Still, I wasn't about to invite Herschel to bring Lucinda over to Julia's for an evening of dinner and conversation. Part of the rationale for not offering Herschel an open invitation dealt with the stolen intimacy between Lucinda and me. I can't imagine how that would turn out if our tryst became the dinner table conversation for the four of us.

But I also realized that Julia and Herschel knew each other. I suspected that they were familiar with each other in a way that could be most disturbing to both Lucinda and me. I won't ask Julia anything about that, though. Frankly, it's none of my business. My connection with Julia is between us and not subject to the influence of others, or at least that's the way I see it for now.

By the same token, Herschel didn't seem to be in a hurry to

invite Julia and me over to his house for an evening of entertainment with him and Lucinda. Herschel did, however, offer to take me fishing. I might just have to do that at some point if the issues between us become more pressing, but I'll not do that now. I really want to focus on settling Grammy's affairs once and for all. I also want to spend as much time alone with Julia as possible.

The more I'm with Julia, though, the more I'm afraid I'll start to tip my hand about my affliction. As much as I might think she'd be accepting of it, I just can't take that chance yet.

Julia's asleep right now. She has the breakfast shift tomorrow. I'll probably just lounge at her house all day while she slaves away at the diner. I think I'll skim through some of her anthropology and psychology books to see if I might find a more illuminated depiction of my affliction than the version that I watched on TV a few nights ago.

# JUNE 9TH

## NEW MOON

Julia and I ate at the diner yesterday. I ordered a half slab of ribs. I felt shaky and nauseous. I hoped that the carnivorous splurge might neutralize my queasiness. It didn't work, though. I had to leave the diner to buy a slab of beef liver from the grocer down the street. I ripped the cellophane from the foam packaging as soon as I exited the store. I had pulled the beef liver from the package when I noticed an old man watching me from the bench next to the store entrance. The urge to suck the blood from the liver tortured me, but I managed to walk down the street a ways and duck into an alley before I indulged in my beef liver lollipop. I thought that my binge on the beef liver would dissolve the thickening paste within my mouth, as well as steady my upset stomach, but it did neither. I'm not sure if this is a matter of tolerance buildup or what. The liver always quelled my blood-thirst before. I just hope that I don't have to seek another source for the blood I crave.

I returned to the grocer with Julia shortly afterwards so that she could buy some salad. I added a few packages of beef liver to her purchase, explaining that I had a peculiar craving for beef liver recently. If this latest batch of liver doesn't curb my blood-thirst, I'm not sure what's next. This poses a problem that I've previously not pondered, and it's a problem that appears much more urgent than any of my other problems. I again felt sickened today. I stayed at Julia's instead of going to town with her. I've already eaten three slabs of beef liver, but my energy seems to have dissipated to the point where it's hard for me to stay focused and active.

Perhaps there's another solution I haven't considered yet. I suppose it's possible that there is some kind of vitamin supplement to offset the blood-thirst and sickness when my craving is not satiated. There might even be some kind of actual medical treatment to address my affliction. Maybe a blood transfusion would do something to appease my condition. I just don't think I could approach a doctor or pharmacist about that yet. I mean, what would I say to the Daniel Boone doctor in town: "Hey, Doc. You got anything to keep me from wanting to suck blood? How about anything to keep me from turning into a werewolf?"

Anyway, I've been reading a few of Julia's anthropology texts during the last two days. I've found some information of interest, but it's really been nothing more useful than to keep my mind from focusing on my worsening nausea. If I am in the worst shape that I can imagine, there is a continuity within the folklore of past cultures that readily accommodates the condition from which I suffer. The actual transformation of human form into that of another creature is an aspect of several belief systems throughout human history. Some of these cultures even regarded a person who was capable of such transformation as a spiritual leader.

But mostly, such a person who is able to shift their shape

was regarded as a monstrosity, an absolute freak of nature who merited extermination to keep from inflicting the damage from the curse upon others who deserved to be spared such a fate. Guess it all boils down to who you hang out with and who you target to appease your blood-thirst.

I'd just assume not validate some ancient belief, either way. I'm not interested in any horrific revival of some beast released from the bondage of the past. I'm quite content to live a normal life if I can figure out how to do that from here. I can pray to the benevolence of this world and universe to spare me from the worst of my plight. I can also delude myself with the belief that I can always act with dignity, regardless of the circumstances that close in on me. I have to cling to this belief that I am good in my heart because I'm sensing more and more that the involuntary is about to possess me again and lead me to complete derangement. The stakes are growing higher, day by day and night by night. If I fail at this endeavor, and, if and when the circumstances dictate, then I'll have to deliberate about my own personal humanity and whether I should continue to live in such a deplorable state of mind and body.

The risk of suffered consequences at this point is wrought with a potential for despair that might warrant such extreme action as suicide, especially if my continued existence is to the ultimate detriment of Julia. After all, she is the only "significant other" really in my life now. I doubt I could live with myself if I destroy Julia in the process, but it's just too problematic for me to say for sure that I will destroy her. I can't kill myself out of fear of what I might do. I'm not even sure I could kill myself for what I'm about to do.

I suppose it might be more beneficial for me to try to delineate the scope of willful action rather than to preoccupy myself with the consequences of incognizant behavior. It's probably a matter of detachment exclusively. After all, actions encompass what is necessity, indulgence, madness, and insanity. It is possible to act with varied degrees of these in simultaneous operation. Hence, detachment separates us from actions that we commit, regardless of the reasons behind the actions. Anything becomes justifiable, regardless of fallacy or illegality. There no longer is any such idealized notion of right or wrong. That is why I must insist upon remaining detached throughout all of this. I must view myself as my own experiment, even if I'm not the one at the controls. Hopefully, this detachment can help me to preserve whatever identity I will have left if I eventually feel like I'm something completely different than myself, or least the self that I've come to know over my three decades here on this earth.

The dream is the other key. I know that I perceive from the perspective of a quadruped in my dream, even though I haven't actually observed the bodily features of my dream body. I also realize that I don't seem to have the capacity for speech in the dream consciousness, which still clearly seems to be my own consciousness and not one belonging to some other entity like an actual animal or a demon. There's something different about the dream consciousness, though. It's like I'm functioning by entirely instinctual means, or at least entrenched in sensory perception alone and not at all influenced by the realm of intellect. The dream consciousness seems to be one of spontaneous generation. It also seems that, at this time, it's also undergoing some kind of transformation that might parallel my own wakeful one within the smokehouse under Grammy's supervision.

I suppose one of the other eggs in my dream might have to hatch before I can rationalize what the dream implies. I'd rather not endow such credence to a dream or bizarre eggs within that dream, but the dream and its surreal landscape are really all I have to gauge what's happening to me while I sleep. If only Grammy would visit me in my dream again and explain what the dream signifies for me, then maybe I could spend my days of wakefulness with enhanced peace of mind.

I've managed to curtail any obsession that the dream might evoke as I mull it over, but my determination not to surrender myself to the dream has weakened over the past two days, just as my physical strength has deteriorated. It's starting to feel like I'm as much at the mercy of this dream as I was at the mercy of the nightmare. The difference is that this dream is more slowly tantalizing than brutally terrorizing like the nightmare was with the Nightmare Eagle assaulting my senses every time I drifted asleep.

Still, it seems wiser to me to address the dream for all that it might signify before some aspect of it changes to paralyze me with dread because I almost fear as much what I'll do in my dream as I fear what I'll do when the inevitable happens and I become a full-fledge werewolf on the prowl in physical form within the actual world.

It's either admit all of this to myself now and prepare for the worst, or I could turn myself into the werewolf prevention authorities. Maybe then I can be restrained by straitjacket and fitted with an electrode helmet to condition the mechanisms of my brain with shocks to the responsible region of wrongheadedness. Of course, I'd be blessed if that's all that I had to endure in the event I did surrender before anything bad happens.

But I'm not going to turn myself in any more than I'm going to kill myself. I'm going to get on with the business of my life, whatever it turns out to be. In that regard, all signs point for me to keep Julia in my thoughts as much as possible right now.

Julia will have Friday and Saturday off work from the diner, but she won't have another day off until June 18<sup>th</sup>, which she informed me is her birthday. She didn't say which birthday, and I didn't ask. I will, however, think about something special to plan for the two of us on her birthday and let her know that I intend to spend the day with her. Of course, for all I know, she's already made other plans, in which case I'll just go with her flow and be glad to have her company.

Julia also disclosed to me that she has vacation time scheduled in July. She didn't divulge any more details about it, but I'm sure we'd be able to coordinate some kind of excursion that would be agreeable for both of us, provided that Julia wants to go out and explore and not just sit on something soft and immerse her feet in a bucket of saltwater. I wouldn't blame her if that's all she wants to do, but if she does want to travel, I'm apparently on an endless vacation for now.

Or maybe I'm just on a sabbatical for the advanced study of werewolvery.

If this latter is the case, then I suppose that this notebook, as well as the other notebooks at Grammy's cabin, will suffice as a doctoral thesis of sorts, even though I don't have so much as an actual bachelor's degree in anything.

I suppose that one of the aspects of this writing that will prove to have importance is the detailed account of the physical condition from which the affliction takes hold. I can feel my saliva froth into paste at the mere thought of blood. It makes me want to hone the fangs in my mind's eye and gash whatever I can find that has blood. I've got it bad, and I'm also out of beef liver. I tried to drink water and orange juice today, but just retched with each sip until I gave up and stopped trying to drink anything.

I have to have blood now. Nothing but blood will do. It's gnawing at my brain and my stomach now without any hope that the urge will abate. The beef liver blood just doesn't seem to be enough. I understand fully that it is human blood that I crave with such consuming force that I'm shaking as I write this.

There has to be a way around this doomed fate, since that's exactly where it looks like I'm headed. "Doomed" probably doesn't accurately describe the future that awaits me. It's actually probably more like I'm cursed and damned by a legacy that I wanted nothing to do with but now find myself hopelessly breathing into life.

I'm about to howl the beast into life and let its fangs rip itself free from my skin.

I have to stop my mind from thinking about this right now. I have far too much time at my disposal to spend all of it chasing my tail like this in such a vicious circle. I need to put down this pen and go outside, if I can make it that far without collapsing. I need to gulp some fresh air to see if that helps at all.

# SUNDAY, JUNE 12TH

## JULIA'S

J ulia didn't just want to lounge around this weekend. She wanted to roam, and I was relieved to join her. The time with Julia did wonders for me physically. I feel much better now.

We browsed the inventory of a couple of used car lots in the area, but I didn't pull the trigger on a purchase. I'll bide my time just a little longer on that front. We then visited Grammy's homestead after our car shopping. Julia absolutely loves the location and the cabin itself. Perhaps her anthropological sensibilities enlivened her with the implications of a lifestyle devoid of basic, modern amenities and any reliance on infrastructure intervention.

Julia didn't even seem to mind the mud daubers that flew from the outhouse when I opened its door. Of course, she might've felt otherwise had they flown up out of the outhouse hole just as she poised her hind end over it. Enough of that experience has given me a lifelong appreciation for the flush of an indoor toilet.

Our visit to Grammy's property did bond Julia and me beyond just the outhouse reality there, though. We seem to have drawn closer, like we're about to really bond in a more lasting way. I feel this urge to gift her something special for her upcoming birthday, but I'm not sure what that would be at this time.

Maybe she'd like some kind of gemstone, even though I've noticed that she doesn't ever wear any kind of jewelry: rings, earrings, bracelets—nothing. She spent considerable time poking around the grounds at Grammy's, looking at rocks and noticing plants and the like there, so maybe she'd like some kind of artifact or something ancient or at least antique. She has a few things like that displayed in her house.

Of course, she probably would prefer something much more practical, like fixing her bedroom ceiling. I can't say I know exactly what's wrong with the ceiling because I've yet to fully enter her bedroom. She did show the room to me from the threshold shortly after she invited me to stay with her. Whatever is wrong with the ceiling wasn't apparent to me during that glimpse of her room. She's mentioned the ceiling a couple of times now. It's probably best to let the landlord deal with the ceiling issue, but I have to wonder if this issue isn't the pretext that I need to join Julia in her bedroom for us to bond more than just drywall mud on her ceiling. Maybe then she'd leave her bedroom door open all of the time instead of keeping it closed.

I probably shouldn't speculate more about Julia's and my future in this respect. As much as she conveys that she's physically attracted to me, I remain hesitant about when and how to pursue her sexually. It seems like timing is the key factor for us to consummate our bond in the most climactic way possible. I certainly feel it building, and she must feel that way also.

A fitting birthday card might also help contribute to the

brewing passion between us. She's received three birthday cards so far that I know of. I watched her smiling as she read them, but then she just unceremoniously deposited them in the kitchen trash can. I suppose I might have displayed them on a counter or shelf somewhere in the house if I were her. This seeming disregard for the whole birthday card sentimentality thing just piques my curiosity about her even more.

I haven't seen Julia receive any gifts yet. Now that would be something if she did receive a birthday gift, only to smile at it before she dumped it into the trash. I guess I'll have to choose my birthday gestures for her wisely.

Of course, the alternative remains out there for a road trip, whether it be somewhere close like the Gorge or a day's drive to somewhere just as naturally awesome, like Mammoth Cave. She'd probably enjoy the latter, but only has one day off. I doubt she'd want to spend that time off driving for most of it.

Then again, a campout at Grammy's might get her juices moving more than anything else. That certainly would be the easiest for both of us, unless, of course, any plan I might make with her is foiled by someone else hosting a birthday party for her. It's not likely that there's a party planned for her, though. She's not exactly flooded with visitors at home or work.

I suppose I still need to buy something for her, regardless of any other activity that might pop up. Unless, of course, that activity involves gnawing on her to the point that I transmit the same legacy to her that Grammy bequeathed to me.

Then, if we shared that affliction, birthday shopping for her would be much easier. I could just give her a package of raw beef liver slabs. God, part of me hopes something like that is possible. I keep waiting for my own fate to be completed in this regard, while at the same time trying to delude myself that I can somehow avoid the worst that it portends. I don't have any doubt that the change is coming for better or worse, and sooner now rather than later. I don't want to be alone when that happens. I'm not sure that anyone trying to live a normal life would want me around in the event I do become completely deranged, but, for some reason, Julia seems to me like someone who might actually have a suitable disposition for tending to a werewolf.

I really don't know why I feel that way toward Julia, but it's true. Something about her suggests to me that we are destined to be together, not just as a man and woman, but in this capacity of whatever it is that is about to take place. Perhaps this is why we were fated to meet: she is going to be my mate.

# JUNE 15TH

## GRAMMY'S CABIN

Herschel told me that he and Lucinda are getting a divorce. That's what he told me when I went to visit him at his house today. His announcement was actually a relief for me, not that I hoped the two would divorce. It's just that I feared the worst since yesterday when Julia told me that Herschel had dropped by the diner in search of me. She said that he had something he wanted to discuss with me, which seemed to concern her for some reason as much as it bothered me.

I envisioned shotgun blasts as I walked from the diner to Herschel's house today, because I thought for sure that this could only be an appointment for me to meet all of Herschel's wrath. I had assumed that Lucinda was once again pregnant with my child and that she had confessed to him that I was the culprit. I expected to be shot, or at least beaten, upon my arrival. I convinced myself that I would accept such a fate for betraying Herschel's friendship once again, but, now, the possibility of my atonement for the home that I've partly wrecked consoles me.

As it turned out, I can now salvage the remnants of the friendship Herschel and I once shared, as well as accept the responsibility for Celeste. I'm not sure how the legal process will unfold in this regard just yet, but I've agreed to pay child support to Lucinda for Celeste's benefit. In some ways, it was a burden relieved to hear Herschel admit that I am Celeste's biological father.

Herschel also remarked that DNA testing would confirm that I am Celeste's father. While he didn't exactly disclose that like it was a threat to me, I understood what he was telling me: it was time for me to take over some of the responsibility for Celeste's upbringing. It feels good, in fact, to have this matter resolved in this way, or at least to have the process to such an end finally initiated. I'll have to consult Lucinda on all of this, though, at a later time. She didn't join us.

From the sound of it, Herschel and Lucinda's divorce will be amicable enough. He just wants to start a new life in Florida, but he did say he and Lucinda had agreed to joint custody of Celeste. He declared that he will always love Celeste like his very own daughter, even if that's not the biological case. I just want to expedite the process for all of us in any way I can.

Before I left Herschel, I blurted a request to him for something that just popped into my mind: if Celeste could join Julia and I for a summer road trip. Of course, Julia doesn't know anything about this yet, but, if I'm to play a significant role in Celeste's upbringing from here on out, I need for her and Julia to get to know each other better, provided, of course, that Julia and I continue to spend more and more time with each other.

So, I really need to let Julia know about this now before her vacation starts in July. If she does have plans already, she hasn't mentioned anything to me about them. It would be fun for the three of us to take a trip, I think. Of course, Julia isn't the only one who would need to know about the travel idea in advance. Celeste would have to be told, as well. It might be too much of a break from her familiarity with Lucinda and Herschel in her life to completely trust Julia and me with her safekeeping on the road for an extended time. I suppose she'd have to be told that I'm her father before she'd feel like such a trip was warranted without Lucinda and Herschel present.

Until I talk this over with Julia, I suppose I'd be better off trying to understand some of my own travel itinerary first: the travel within my dream, that is. I'd really like to remain here at Grammy's cabin for a while to see if she has any information in her cabin that might help me with my lycanthropic predicament. Perhaps she wrote a journal and hid it somewhere in the cabin. As much as I'd like to examine the contents of the cabin, I won't do so until the will is read. I am going to spend the night here, which probably will cause some concern for Julia. I just don't feel like trudging all the way back to town right now, plus I have no way to contact her. Hopefully, Julia won't worry too much.

I must admit that I've enjoyed the solitude and am looking forward to more by staying here tonight. Undoubtedly, too much time here might drive me out of my mind, but, for now, this is an ideal setting for someone who has to wax with the moon, so to speak. No wonder Grammy stayed here. She had to go to town for various matters, and, obviously, she had to see doctors there, but she remained here at the cabin property all the same over all of those years,

Her visits with doctors and hospitals begs the question, though, about whether others knew about her affliction. Surely, if Grammy experienced cellular mutation at the level required for the lycanthropic transformation, that trauma would leave some kind of medical mark, both internal and external, that would not escape the attention of the medical profession.

Perhaps she did leave some record here in the cabin of the physiological details of her affliction. I doubt I'll be so lucky to discover that she wrote a journal about it, but anything that might shed some light on this for me would be greatly appreciated. None of the books in Grammy's bookcase suggest anything that might help illuminate the mystery of my affliction. There are only the Poe volumes that were always there from the time of my childhood.

I had hoped that my ongoing dream might provide more insight about my condition for me, but much of what transpires in the dream just seems to deepen the mystery:

I awoke from the dream last night in the den beneath the narrow slab of rock bridge. I ascended the cliff to the bridge, then I paused at the realization that I was standing in snow next to the nest. I also see that the hollow below the ridge is now snow-covered. I soon returned my attention to the nest and climbed it. I observed the same scene as before: the two remaining eggs were unhatched beside the fragments of the shell from which Grammy hatched.

I descended from the nest back to the rock bridge. That's when I noticed the footprint in the snow, leading away from the nest. It is that of a small, bare foot, undoubtedly like Grammy's foot. But how? She hatched and left before any snowfall.

I assume that she has come back to the nest for some reason, as I scan for more tracks in the snow. I find the next footprint. It, too, is leading away from the nest. The print is sharp and firm. I know it is Grammy's foot that has left this recently formed mark. I whimper in my reluctance to leave the safety of the rock bridge. The prints end at the edge of the ridge, which means that Grammy descended the steep slope below the ridge that unfolds to the snow-covered hollow below. I'm too afraid to follow, so I don't. Instead, I return to my dream den below the rock slab of bridge and curl myself there to go back to sleep within my dream.

But all of that will have to wait now.

I see a flashlight coming toward the cabin.

Somebody thinks enough of me to brave the dusk and isolation here to pay me a visit within these spooky old woods.

I'm just hopeful that it's Julia. I have my camping gear here with me, so maybe she's willing to spend the night with me here. Maybe then we can have the kind of talk we really need to have in regard to how we fit into each other's plans.

But if it's not Julia, then I must get myself ready.

And that means I need to get Grammy's old revolver from the cabin.

Or maybe I'll pass on the gun. I need a shootout right now like I need a hole in the head.

# JUNE 16TH

## GRAMMY'S CABIN

How glad I was to see Julia last night! I met her on the path to the porch. She had a small cooler with her, which she set on the ground as I approached her. When I reached her, we hugged each other cheek to cheek long enough to engorge me from our embrace. She laughed a little before she disengaged the hug. I then kissed her lips before she told me that she had something to drink for me in the cooler. I grabbed the cooler, then led her by the hand up the steps to Grammy's porch.

I motioned for Julia to sit on the porch rocking chair. I sat on the porch floor with my feet on the steps, then I opened the cooler, handing one cold can of sweet iced tea to her and taking the other for myself. We sipped our tea as we conversed mostly about the property. When the subject veered toward the books inside of Grammy's cabin, Julia wanted to see for herself.

That's when the revelation came like a bolt of lightning from the Poe anthology that Julia opened: Grammy's copy of **Tales of the Grotesque and Arabesque** had a piece of paper inside marking the page for the start of the Poe short story, *"William Wilson."*

I had read through this volume many times, never pondering its value. Julia was quite dramatic about how this was an original from 1840 and probably worth an absolute fortune. She calmed down long enough to take the paper note that served as a bookmark. She then read to me the name and the address of the person written on it with an additional note from Grammy, "If you ever get this, go see your mother. She lives in Ensenada, Mexico and is expecting you."

I couldn't believe my eyes. I thought my mother was either dead or long gone out of my life for good with her own life far away from here. But this suddenly seemed to change everything for me. I explained to Julia what this note meant. She was now even more amazed by her rare book find and the unfathomable note within it. As I stood stupidly staring at the note, Julia suggested that maybe we should take a road trip to Mexico to visit my mother.

Julia and I sat at the kitchen table lit by lantern light for the next few hours. Her first interest was the rare Poe book, but she soon asked me questions about who my mother was, what I remembered about her, why I had left for Europe, and how Grammy had managed to live in these woods and cabin. We finally reached a point where sleepiness crept into both of us.

Julia suggested that we sleep in the cabin, but I had to tell her that the only bed here was Grammy's old bed. I told her that I had changed the sheets the last time I was here. I also told her that the mattress seemed cleaned and relatively newer. We went into the bedroom for her to have a look and feel of the bed. She said it seemed fine to her, so we crawled into bed beneath the cover, sharing the pillow for a while before she shifted her face to my bare chest.

I stroked Julia's arm and back for a while, wondering if we were about to consummate our physical attraction right then and there, but we didn't. She was exhausted and fell asleep. I was tired, too, and didn't have to wait much longer before I also drifted into sleep.

I fell straight into the dream. This time I followed Grammy's tracks, determined in my sleeping consciousness to find her now that I know she left me this message about my mother. I struggled through deep snow to track her, not knowing where I was going or how far I had traveled. I became alarmed, fearful that I was being lured away from the den. I scanned the cloudless but lightless black sky for maybe some other Nightmare Eagle, but none was anywhere to be seen. I whimpered in fear of going forward before I backtracked in my dream body.

I was exhausted in my dream by the time I reached the rock bridge. I shakily scaled down the dream den on the ledge, where I curled into my sleeping position and immediately returned to sleep within my dream.

I know that Grammy lurks out there somewhere within my dream, waiting for me to reach her. It's unclear to me what she can reveal to me or why I have to trudge on all fours through deep snow to search for her, but I know that eventually I'll pursue her farther within my dream.

As much as I'd love to reunite with Grammy in the dream realm, I'd also like to see my mother again in the real world. I never had any intent to pursue my mother before, but, now that it seems more or less ordained by the message from Grammy, I believe I'm ready to travel to find my mother. I just don't how to contact her yet. I'll have to find a phone number for her.

Julia has yet to wake. When she does, I'll see if she wants to join me for an outing to Winchester today. I believe it's high time I went to visit my old friend Virgil at the sporting goods store to see if I can't repay him for his kindness to me and pick up some more gear for my extended road trip to Mexico.

Of course, I'll have to borrow Julia's car if she wants to go to work instead of taking her lunch shift off today. Or maybe I'll just go buy my own car. Funny how all of the sudden I seem to have more purpose and feel like I'm going to be more decisive about what I do. I hope this resurgent confidence doesn't leave Julia behind, though. I really enjoyed having her body next to mine last night, even though we kept our clothes on the whole night.

There's always tonight for our disrobing, I guess.

But, now, I hear Julia stirring in the bedroom. Time for me to go greet her, so that we can get this day started.

# JUNE 16TH

## JULIA'S

It's been a long day, but I want to write this down now. Julia allowed me the use of her car today, and I drove to Winchester to meet Virgil. Not only did I buy road trip camping gear, I also bought a used car for $5,200. I actually drove all the way back here with Virgil following me in his truck to withdraw the money for the car, then we returned to Winchester in his truck to buy the car. It's a four-door hatchback that should have plenty of room for two adults, one child, and gear for a week's worth of travel. More importantly, the car has 75,000 thousand miles on it, so it should be good for a cross-country trip, at least Virgil seems to think so.

I almost didn't get underway this morning. Julia greeted me with a long kiss when she woke up. The fragrant and tasty funk of her mouth and tongue instantly aroused me. We lavished each other with several more kisses and seemed destined for passionate lovemaking on Grammy's bed, but I suppressed my lust for her by mentioning the use of her car.

Julia was glad to help, but she told me that I'd have to pay her back on her birthday in her bedroom instead of Grammy's. That's the day after tomorrow. I said I'd have her present ready.

In the meantime, I'll finalize insurance for my new car tomorrow, then I'll prepare myself to deliver Julia's birthday present. After Julia's birthday, I don't have anything planned until the reading of Grammy's will, which I learned today at the bank is set for the end of June. There's a full moon in between now and then on the 23$^{rd}$, so it remains to be seen what that brings for me.

By the time I returned here to Julia's house from Winchester, Julia was already asleep, so I'll tell her about the car tomorrow. Now, it's time for me to get some sleep, too.

# JUNE 18TH

## JULIA'S

The moon accelerates and beckons me for a rendezvous with it. Before much longer, the moon will broadcast the entirety of its skeletal beam and rip this old skin from me so I can bulge from the rage of liberation. Even now as my hands throb and shake, static sparks at my fingers.

The first burst of energy came through my eyes. I see more depth than ever before. I have an almost zoom lens capability for vision now. I can even shift my focus so that what I see is either magnified microscopically or retracted to present an amazingly wider field of view.

Different stimuli produce a colorful array of lit dots that I can control and condense into a single minuscule beam of vision that illuminates whatever it falls up within the darkness outside. This all seems to me like the proof that I'm about to burst from the inside. My transitioning must be just about complete. I suppose the enhanced vision is preparation for the nocturnal odyssey that undoubtedly awaits me. My eyes are now the filters through which the merger of dream and reality defies diffraction with the absolute gleam of the aurora in front of me and inside of me.

I feel so energized with life now, too. Julia and I went to the Gorge for her birthday today. She requested the trip, and I was happy to oblige. We covered several miles on foot in the afternoon. She struggled to keep up with me. I tried not to leave her behind, but I felt like some chained mongrel freed from its restraints.

By the conclusion of our jaunt through the Gorge, Julia was sopped with sweat. She never complained about my rapid pace. In fact, I think she rather enjoyed the exertion. Our excursion did exhaust her, though. When we returned to her house, she immediately staggered her way to her bedroom and dropped to the bed, leaving her clothes on and her door open. So much for giving her a proper birthday present tonight.

As for me, I've remained excruciatingly awake. Right now, I'm fighting the urge to return to Gorge even as I write this, so that I can run free through its wilderness at night. This surge of clarity and vitality is intoxicating. I have to treat it as such and not succumb to the urges I now feel circulating within me. I haven't felt this exhilarated about what comes next since I was a teenager on a plane for London.

The changes aren't only happening to me while awake. The expedition of my dream body far exceeded my previous clamber through the snow. I didn't locate Grammy last night, but I did traverse deeply into what seems to me like familiar territory. If I can manage to detect some landmark in the dream realm that corresponds to a real landmark that I actually recognize, then I'd be able to establish some coordinates to pursue during wakeful daylight hours.

I've never slept more soundly. This resurgence of mind and body during daylight hours might have a lot to do with the restoration of the deep sleep that I've enjoyed immeasurably. Funny, too, that my dream expedition in the snow also seems to refresh me for my reawakening once my prolonged slumber is over.

I feel like I'm at the threshold of the prowl now, both when awake and asleep.

But, in the meantime, I have to bide my time and appetite with raw beef liver and oyster crackers. Just like Grammy did during her life as a shapeshifting werewolf.

I'm determined to continue my search for Grammy within my dream, and, when I find her, I can only hope that I intuit what the intersection of dream with reality signifies. Perhaps even the distinction between the body in life and the mind after death will dissolve.

Dawn is coming now. I have some sleeping to do now.

# TUESDAY, JUNE 21ST

## SUMMER SOLSTICE AT GRAMMY'S CABIN

What better way to spend the longest day of the year than holed up here at Grammy's? Julia worked double shifts the past two days since her birthday, so I drove my car here and decided to spend all of yesterday and last night on the grounds. I've spent most of the daylight hours pining for Julia's air conditioning because it's been a real swelter.

Yesterday was as uneventful as today was for me. It's been a chance to relax despite the heat and smothering humidity. My sleep, however, is a much different story. I'm starting to feel like I'm just trying to get through the day to fall asleep so I can see where my dream will go.

The dream leads me farther into the woods than ever. I've managed to blaze my trail through the snow, though, so I know how to get back to my dream den beneath the rock bridge. It's become easier to navigate my way deeper into the snowy woods, and I'm not exhausted by the time I return any longer. I haven't encountered anything other than Grammy's single-foot track in the snow and the snow-blanketed woods during this nocturnal dream journey, but my acuity seems to sharpen with every four-legged step forward. I feel so aware and alive in my dream that I have to wonder if this isn't some kind of training that prepares me for whatever might lunge at me out of this silvery darkness. The full moon is only a few days away. The nocturnal light will beam stranger yet.

One aspect of the dream has become so bizarre: the farther I progress into the woods, the more I thirst for blood. I've licked the snow to draw its moisture, but this only aggravates the blood-thirst and creates more paste within my mouth. Fortunately, the blood-thirst is now a feature of my dream alone and not my waking life. I'm craving blood less when awake in the world of daylight, and my actual thirst is more readily quenched by normal drinks now than ever before since Grammy bit me.

I have to deduce that I must satiate this blood-thirst at some point in my dream. What rapacious snatch this will require, I'm afraid to guess. I just hope that the attack remains within the realm of dream and doesn't somehow extend into the world of the awake and the living. The last thing I want is for the hunt within my dream to conclude with my waking up in bed next to the bloodied, mutilated corpse of Julia.

But I won't succumb to any paranoid conclusions just yet. The evidence suggests otherwise. The long life of Grammy tells me there's a way through this without the direst of consequences. Whatever core of decency exists within me must spare me of my morbid fate and sustain me throughout this unreal ordeal.

Hopefully, my dream body will feel the same. I find myself feeling a certain tenderness for the hope of a reunion with Grammy, even while I know I'm pursuing some end that results in satiation of the blood-thirst at the expense of some living creature. Perhaps this is the most lasting gift of Grammy's legacy: her kindness toward me during her life has now detoured the obstruction of death to find me once again in need of her selfless love for me.

I suppose it's only natural for someone to think about a loved one who has recently passed away, but the recurrence of this dream is an undertow of a confluence beyond anything that I'm equipped to comprehend. The intense psychic energy that prevails in the dream seeks Grammy in physically viable form. This can't have anything to do with grief. It's more like she's teaching me again, guiding my psyche through the otherworldly landscape.

But I do have to remember to caution myself about my affinity for Grammy. She was the one, after all, who bit me. Granted that put an end to the assaults by the Nightmare Eagle, but it's still left me stranded here, afflicted in this plight.

I suppose at the end of the day, or dream, rather, that the proof will be in the pudding. Of course, in my case, the pudding looks like it will be blood, and I'm afraid there will be lots of it. If there is a moral in all of this for me, it has to have everything to do with the pudding. Gluttony would just be sadistic. As much as the sheer carnal pang of my dream body consumes me while asleep, I have to try to resist any urge to regress into some bestial feeding frenzy that is depraved beyond measure. The last thing I need is to be the target of attention if I do end up leaving a trail of mutilation behind me.

Even in the face of this werewolvery, I have to believe that kindness can prevail somehow. At one moment, it is possible to gnaw flesh from bone, then at another it's quite a sincere gesture when the wound of another is licked by a tongue hinged from kindness.

Perhaps all that I really can do is persist with my mantra of kindness, even as I continue to regress within my dream body toward the completion of my transformation. I might become hopelessly primordial in my beastly conversion, but that doesn't mean I have to forego some primordial occurrence of kindness that the human heart can selflessly impart upon all life. This might seem hopelessly idealistic, but the extremes are so exaggerated in my instance now that the choice that awaits me has to be what I interpret from what is lodged like a fang in what might as well be called a soul.

This may prove to be my only salvation.

This may be the last vestige of me that truly remains human.

# DATE UNKNOWN

## "FULL MOON SIPHONS SOULS WITH BEAMS OF PULL"

I awoke on the porch, bloodied and naked. The blood wasn't mine, though, and I'm ambivalent about how I came to wear it beneath the radiance of the full moon.

I was wide awake at Julia's when the dream somehow externalized and I transformed into the beast. It just happened, which turned out to be good timing because Julia was asleep on the couch when I changed my skin.

I thought I was having problems with my eyes when the change started. I ran into the hallway bathroom and tried to wipe the exploding dots of lights from my eyes. The more I tried to stop the dots from exploding, the more nauseous I became until I finally started to retch over the bathroom sink.

When it was obvious that I couldn't stop what was happening to me, I stumbled out of the bathroom and staggered down the hallway toward the kitchen, where I lunged for the door to the back porch. Once outside on the porch, I struggled to negotiate the steps to the backyard, where I then collapsed in the grass.

But instead of impacting the hard ground, I somehow spun right through the impact into some kind of spatial medium devoid of the physical world where I just had been. When the spinning stopped, I opened my eyes to discover that I was face first on the ledge of my dream den below the rock slab of bridge.

It took me a minute to orient myself. I tried to stand at first but realized I couldn't lift myself to my feet. I then proceeded to climb on all fours from the ledge, just like I would do in my dream. Only this time, I didn't pursue Grammy's tracks. Instead, I scaled the nest until I reached its top. When I peered into the nest, I whimpered at the sight of one remaining egg: the fragments of the other egg were strewn across the fragments from the egg that had hatched Grammy.

As soon as I realized that something else had hatched from the other egg, I leapt from the nest to the bridge to begin my search for another set of footprints. The footsteps followed the trail that Grammy had left with her one foot. This other person who had hatched left the bridge on two feet. I lunged down the valley on the other side of the ridge in pursuit of the fresh tracks. With each burst forward, the blood-thirst further maddened me. I knew I was on the hunt to satiate it.

Then I froze in my own tracks when I heard the howl ahead of me. It had to be Grammy, or else it was whoever this other hatch was. Part of me feared for Grammy's safety as I resumed my race down the hill. I don't know how long I pursued the trail at my utmost speed. I didn't even slow down when I noticed the changes to the ground beneath me: the snow turned to slush that turned to mud, which in turn became grass-covered, hard earth.

Although I lost the tracks of Grammy and the other hatched entity, I nevertheless maintained connection to their scents. I was close to the source of those smells, but I was also suddenly aware of something else. I recognized a landmark as one that was within the Red River Gorge. I was more alarmed by the familiar scenery than I was apprehensive about my looming encounter with whoever awaited me at the end of my jaunt through the dream world that had somehow turned real. I maintained my speed in pursuit, not at all tired by the exertion that seemed to have lasted for over an hour.

But I froze immediately at the sound of a detonation that could only have been a shotgun blast above the precipice ahead of me. I stayed frozen as I waited for something else to happen, which did when another disruption startled me. Something heavy tore through tree branches in its fall from the top of the cliff, and then it hit the ground floor of the Gorge with such a thud that I felt the vibrations beneath my all fours. Only after a considerable silence did I warily approach the point of impact.

When I reached the scene, the hairs on my nape stood straight up. There in front of me was a creature that had its back to me as it hunkered over a mangled mass beneath it. When the creature hopped on one hind leg, I knew that I had found Grammy. I wanted to scamper to her and lick her, but I instead approach even more warily than before.

Grammy turned her snout toward me. Her glazed eyes gazed blindly at me, but she knew who I was. She whimpered as I inched forward. Her remarkable presence there wasn't enough to deter me from the smell of the blood that I could see pooled around the crumpled mass beneath her.

I could see the twisted, nude victim. Grammy hopped away from the dead body as I approached. Nothing could keep me from doing what I was about to do, which was to gorge myself upon the meat of the fresh corpse and appease my crazed bloodthirst.

The pool of blood around the body glistened in the full

moonlight. I lapped the blood-soaked hair upon the head of the victim. I licked the blood away then pawed at the head, turning its lifeless weight until I could see the features of the person's face. I recognized the open eyes. The familiarity of the man's scent further identified him for me.

It was Julia's dentist friend.

The recognition compelled me to pause from my heinous activity. I lifted my head to entreat Grammy to explain what had happened, but the wolf with one back leg was gone. The hunger redirected my attention back to the dead man. I didn't even try to resist what thoroughly sickens me now. I tore at the man's flesh and lapped his blood. My only consolation for what I did was that the man was already dead. He was a fresh kill who had met his untimely demise without any direct cause from me.

Only after I had quelled the vile hunger within me did I think about Julia's dentist friend somewhat more humanely. Clearly, he had been murdered, and that fact needed to be brought to the light of day. I could see that the shotgun slug had entered his chest and then exploded out of his back, but that wasn't all that had been done to him. There was a metal rod that looked like a crowbar that had been shoved up his rectum. It also looked like his wrists were bound behind his back with some kind of plastic ties.

Whatever problems that the dentist might have caused for others, and regardless of the justification that someone might claim for revenge, the dentist didn't deserve such evil treatment. A sense of justice did not escape me then. While I most definitely wasn't proud of my feeding upon the body, I most certainly was proud of my decision at that point. I decided to drag the dentist's body to a place where it would be more readily discovered.

I didn't expect the transport of the body to be as difficult as it was, though. I had to clamp one of his feet with my jaws and proceed backwards, dragging what was left of the dentist along as I went. Despite the energy I exerted, I still didn't tire, and when I finally dragged the body all the way up a hill to a road that circled the Gorge, I was amazed that I was still invigorated enough to start my journey back to the dream den.

My return trip, however, was much more difficult than the pursuit of the dream trail had been. What made it worse was that I didn't encounter snow again, so I couldn't backtrack like I had done all of those other times in my dream journey. I would feel lost until I looked up at the full moon, then I would feel it pull me in the direction that I needed to go. The moon didn't fail me. Despite the eventual exhaustion of my transformed dream body, I was elated when my claws clacked across the deck boards of Grammy's porch. Dawn was approaching when I plopped on the porch and fell asleep within the dream that had turned too real.

The hot morning sun would awaken me soon enough, though. It was like I hadn't slept at all, and I could barely move. Even though I was naked and bloody on the porch, I stayed there for at least a couple hours, trying to recuperate enough just to get to my feet. The overexertion from my dream journey had rendered me so agonizingly sore that it was all that I could do to reach this notebook on the porch table.

I'll have to find some clothes here before I try to walk to my car. I left a pair of shorts and a T-shirt in Grammy's bedroom chest. I just wonder how Julia will react to me vanishing like this, only to return in a clearly altered state. I'm not sure that I can hide this change in me from her, but at least I can wash off here with well water before I leave for her house.

There's also the murder of the dentist. I don't see how I can report it to the police, but I don't think that would be necessary anyway. I brought the body where it could be found, and I don't know anything about who killed him or why. Besides, I must have left teeth marks on his body. I'm not sure those teeth I used to tear him apart would match the ones in my mouth right now, but I don't want to risk finding that out.

Now, there's the issue of this writing, too. It does incriminate me. This notebook is nearly full, so I suppose it is best for me to hide what I've written. Or maybe I'd be better off if I burnt all of it. No. I won't do that. At least not yet.

And there is one other thing I have to consider. What if the dentist had some blood transmittable disease, like AIDS or hepatitis? Does that mean that I am also at risk to contract what he had, since I ate him and lapped up most of his blood, after all?

I suppose that will all have to wait until the situation starts to clear itself up.

# SUNDAY, JUNE 26TH

## "THE POWER OF THE SPIRIT SHREDS THE FLESH AWAY"

It is Sunday, June 26<sup>th</sup>. I'm writing this at Julia's house. She's off work today but has spent most of her time on the phone talking to people about her dead dentist friend. When she told me about his death, I tried to feign as much surprise as I could muster. Any type of movement, though, just makes me wince, and I nearly shrieked in pain in response to her news.

Julia asked me what was wrong with me. I lied that I had tweaked a back muscle and found it hard to breathe, much less move. I'm just glad she was at work yesterday when I was finally able to return to her house from Grammy's. Since Julia worked a double shift yesterday, she really didn't have the time or energy to ask about why I wasn't at her house the night before.

Now, the news of her dentist friend's death seems to have gotten me off the hook in that regard. She handed the front-page section of the Lexington newspaper to me while she talked on the phone. I shuffled to the kitchen with paper in hand then read the article, which detailed the grisly discovery of the dentist's body in the Red River Gorge. The homicide investigation was in full swing, and the article concluded with the inclusion of information that coyotes or wild dogs had mauled the nude body of the dentist.

After I read the article, I was amazed by one fact that wasn't included in the newspaper: I had somehow managed to traverse fifty miles upon all fours in a time of less than seven hours. No wonder I can hardly move. At least I had a change of clothes and made it back to Julia's from Grammy's in my car yesterday.

Julia had finally approached me as I sat at the kitchen table. She scooted the other chair beside me then sat. She hooked her arm with mine before she placed her cheek on my shoulder and started to cry. I wanted to stroke her hair and caress her neck but couldn't lift my arm without pain. So, I just let her sob and squeeze my arm.

When Julia finished crying, she told me that she and the dentist had been engaged to be married at one point. He was the reason she had moved to this area. I had suspected something along these lines existed in the relationship between them. I told her that I was sorry about her loss, but that I would do whatever I could to help her.

That's when she asked me to join her in her bed. She said she didn't want to be alone tonight. She then lifted her face from my shoulder and met my gaze with her big, teary eyes. I could tell that she just didn't want me in bed beside her. She wanted me sexually, which she then wordlessly confirmed for me by, first, reaching the button and, then, the zipper of my shorts. I struggled to lift myself high enough off of the chair so that she could pull down my shorts. I wasn't wearing any underwear, so I was all out in her full view before she could slide my shorts past my knees.

Julia pounced me with her mouth as she shoved me back

down into the chair. I groaned in pain as I maneuvered the shorts over my knees and down to my ankles so that she could position herself between my legs. I felt the spasms of cramps forming in my hamstrings, but I shifted my weight forward enough to keep my muscles from seizing. Despite my efforts, there just wasn't any way for me to overcome the mounting spasms that were about to debilitate me.

My body jerked when the hamstrings seized. I cried in pain, pushing Julia from me before I flung myself to the floor. I yelled that my hamstrings were cramped. She came to me and massaged my legs, assuring me that I would be all right. I told her that I was sorry, and I'd be ready next time we engaged. She said she'd be ready, too. After a lengthy massage, she finally helped me to her bed, and we went to sleep. I hope to have better luck next time.

# WEDNESDAY JUNE 29TH

## "THE MOON-EYED DWELLERS IN DARKNESS HAVE A FRIEND IN THE NIGHT"

It's Wednesday, June 29th. I'm at Herschel and Lucinda's house. Well, actually it's just Lucinda's house now. The backyard wilderness shrieks with the cacophony of cicadas. I remember that darkened day when the last cicada swarm unleashed its unearthed ascent. Clouds of cicadas everywhere. These noisy ones of summer aren't the same as their swarming cousins, who periodically escape nymphal imprisonment underground to obscure the light of day with their upheaval.

Undoubtedly, poor little Celeste must feel like she's caught in the middle of a locust swarm about now. Her life is all about upheaval now. I'm not sure how wise it was for Lucinda to reveal to Celeste that I am her father, but the cicadas are out of the bag, so to speak.

Lucinda drove to Julia's house today while Julia was at work. Her knock at the door took me off guard. When I opened the door, I was immediately afraid of what Lucinda and I were going to do. Another lustful episode between us wasn't in the works, though, in large part because Lucinda was distraught when she delivered the news that Herschel had left her for good after the two of them had a fight that left her with several bite marks.

The mention of bites pretty much froze me. I stood stunned at the threshold as Lucinda turned her bandaged forearm toward me.

As much as I wanted to ask her if Herschel was a wolf when he bit her, I didn't, but I really didn't have to ask her that. I could see the terror in her eyes that what she encountered was more than just Herschel.

I knew I needed to get Lucinda back to her house where we could talk much more freely. I wasn't about to let Lucinda inside of Julia's house, anyway. Julia would be coming home soon. She was getting off work early to meet a detective involved with the homicide investigation of her dentist friend. Apparently, the police think that Julia might be able to provide information that could help find whoever was responsible for her friend's death.

So, I told Lucinda that we needed to go to her house instead. I followed her in my car and came here to her house. She first furnished me with all the details about her wounds caused by Herschel's bite, then she told me about the bite that Herschel had suffered a few years ago. Apparently, the bite Herschel suffered had come from something much different than just a dog.

I could see that Lucinda wanted to tell me that Herschel had transformed into something other than human when he bit her, but I steered her away from any urge to disclose that to me. I just don't want to know at this point. Plus, I couldn't risk letting her know about my own affliction. Instead, I pulled her to me on the couch and let her sob for a while until she calmed down enough to tell me the next piece of news: Celeste finding out that I am her father.

Lucinda had already informed me that Celeste wasn't in the house. She was visiting her grandparents for the day. I asked Lucinda if Celeste was present during Herschel's attack. Lucinda said she was spending the night with her grandparents that night, so at least she was spared that much of this whole ordeal.

I finally put Lucinda to bed. She asked me to join her, but I said that I really had to return to Julia's house for a pressing matter. She asked me what was wrong, but I said I couldn't say. I left her bedroom then left a note for her on her nightstand that I would contact her soon. She is exhausted right now and needs rest more than anything else. I'd better head out for my next pow wow of the day with Julia. Hopefully, she's all finished with the police.

"WHOSOEVER SHALL WITNESS THE
ARRIVAL OF THIS CREATURE SHALL
FEAST UPON ITS FREEDOM. SHOULD
ITS FANGS SINK INTO YOUR HEART,
REST ASSURED ALL SORROW SHALL
DEPART."

It is Thursday, June 30th. I'm here at Grammy's cabin, which is to say, my cabin now.

A pitcher of well water sweats on the table beside me as I sit on my porch, and I have to admit that it does taste a little more refreshing now that the property from which it was drawn is legally my own.

I went to the cemetery for the first time since Grammy's burial. I suppose I could've gone earlier to pay my respects, but it's not exactly like I really consider Grammy to be dead. Perhaps in the real world, but not at all in my dream realm.

So, I did go to the cemetery today with Julia after we went to the bank to hear Grammy's will read. Her headstone is small. The "Rest in Peace" epitaph is concise. According to the dates of birth and death, Grammy lived a long life of ninety-four years. I owe her a debt of eternal gratitude, but I might have to spend the rest of my life paying for that with this mordacious legacy she has bequeathed to me.

As for the last will and testament, that was actually the

simplest event I've experienced in a while. All I had to do was sign the will and a few other documents, then the property and cabin were legally mine. I suppose now that I'm financially solvent once again and situated with a place of my own in this world, I should celebrate. What better way to do that than a road trip across the country to Mexico?

I mentioned as much to Julia after we returned to her house from our day together. She's all in. She's so enthusiastic, in fact, that I was somewhat taken aback. I then blurted to her that I'd like to drive to South Padre Island in Texas. I quickly added that we could travel to San Diego from there, which would give us a straight shot south through Tijuana to Ensenada.

I didn't explain that the reason I wanted to go to South Padre was the remotest possibility that I might somehow rendezvous with the Girl from Ohio who I encountered at the Gorge upon my return to Kentucky. I'll have to find out when she'll be there, though. I remember her saying she would be in South Padre in July. I still have her contact info, so I might have to call her soon.

The more Julia and I discussed the itinerary, the clearer it became that this would be a two-week vacation road trip. Julia asked me if I had contacted my mother. I told her that I only had her address so far, to which Julia asked what we would do if we drove all the way to Ensenada and missed her. I replied that we would just have to enjoy Ensenada to ourselves.

But I suppose I do need to contact my mother before we leave for this trip.

Of course, I mentioned nothing about my nocturnal anomaly to Julia at this point. Wouldn't want to put the buzz kill in our road trip plans, but so far since my last lycanthropic excursion, I haven't even seemed to wake up within my dream.

I didn't mention anything about Celeste joining us, either.

That could prove to be another fly in the ointment for Julia. I hope not. I returned to Kentucky about three months ago, and it's been a bunch of chaos. Hitting the road with Julia and Celeste might make me feel more normal than I have for a long while.

Plus, I've never traveled out west before. I've been throughout Western Europe and spent far too many years in the middle of Rome, but the farthest west I've ever been is the westernmost boundary of the Ohio River. I'd say it's about time I headed west for a while.

# SUNDAY, JULY 3RD

## "ITS GLIMMER IN THE DISTANCE EMBARKS FROM ITS EYES. THE WILDERNESS ENTREATS ITS WILL TO SURVIVE."

I'm at Julia's now on this Sunday, July 3rd, the day before Independence Day, and what could be a better day than that to get ready for a road trip to Mexico.

The executor of Grammy's will notified me on Friday that there was one other matter to settle with Grammy's estate. It involved access to her PO Box and safety deposit box at the bank. Turns out the latter contained several gold coins and the telephone number to reach my mother in Ensenada, where she remarried and now lives with her current husband, Rodrigo.

I talked with my mother for quite some time. She said she already knew about Grammy's passing. She also said that she had been expecting my call. She had a lot of questions for me, and I had many for her. However, she wouldn't answer my questions about the lycanthropic legacy bequeathed to me. She said she had to be present with me before she could tell me everything I would need to know.

So, we set a date for a place south of Ensenada called La Bufadora, which is apparently some kind of marine geyser that warrants its Spanish name of "blowhole." I'm supposed to reunite with my mother there on July 18th. I feel anxious about this meeting, but I'm also very energized by the prospect. Even though I don't really need my mother in my life, I'm still endeared to her in ways that compel me to think lovingly toward her.

Julia is also revved up for this trip, especially now that Ensenada has been confirmed. This is the most excited that I've seen her since we started seeing each other. She kisses and hugs me a lot more openly now, and we hold hands when we're together in town. We'd undoubtedly be sexually rampant with each other if it weren't for her insistence that we wait a little longer before we consummate our passion for each other in the utmost intimate way.

When I asked her why the reluctance, she tells me that she wants the next time she is with a man to mean the world to her and her partner. She wants it to be the kind of coupling that is a binding commitment to be together from that time forward.

I suppose I respect that, although the wait for me can be excruciating at times. Fortunately, Julia isn't averse to appeasing my sexual appetite in other ways, which I must say she has performed most satisfyingly for me twice since my hamstring episode rendered me helpless last week.

So, I'll honor Julia's wishes. That means I'm not going to try to be with any other woman, whether it be Lucinda or the Girl from Ohio, should I cross paths with the latter in South Padre Island during my trip. The chances of me and the Girl from Ohio being together are virtually nonexistent, anyway, now, since I've decided not to contact her.

Julia is also on board with Celeste joining us for the trip. I told Julia that I've been informed that I am Celeste's biological father. She thought it was sweet that I wanted to take her with us on the trip. She added that she thought I would make a good father.

Lucinda is also on board with Celeste going on the trip. She has placed Celeste with her grandparents for the time being. I plan on visiting Celeste soon to discuss the details of the trip with her. I'm not sure what I'll need in the way of legal documentation to serve as her guardian for this trip. I could be opening up a huge can of worms by taking her with us. She could pout and gripe the whole time, or something could happen to her medically or otherwise that could put her in more jeopardy with me than if she was on a road trip with Lucinda or Herschel.

I'm going to chance it, though. It's bound to be an adventure for all three of us.

# 4TH OF JULY

## "THE LIGHT SHOWERS DOWN WITH SPARKS THAT SURPRISE."

C an't say I've spent a worse Fourth of July than this one. I'm in Julia's bathroom writing this now. I have to be near a toilet. What's been disgorged from me can't just be left heaped around. Whatever this vomit is made of, it sure looks like the ugliest mixture of blood and meat chunks that I've ever seen. The abdominal cramps that seize me before each discharge are excruciating. The blood-thirst is over-whelming me again, too, and no matter what I do, I can't seem to quench it. I can't even eat raw beef liver now. The mere smell of it induces more vomiting.

Fortunately, Julia hasn't been here to hear me puking my guts out. She'd likely call an ambulance if she saw and smelled this unholy mess that I'm spewing. Julia's down the street at a neighbor's house watching fireworks. Hopefully, she won't come back until this wretched episode of mine is finished.

I've tried everything I could think of to stop this violence within me. Writing all of this down is my last resort. I'm writing as fast as I can to take my mind off my condition. It seems to be working so far.

The dream resumed last night. I awoke within the den and cried from physical pain. Brutal spasms seized my entire body. My bowels and bladder emptied. All I could do was try to escape my own offal. I managed to fight through my pain to scale the rocky slope to the slab of bridge above me. I climbed the nest and peered inside: one egg remained amidst the strewn fragments of the other two that have hatched. I peered closer over the side of the nest and sniffed as deeply as I could to get some sense of who or what is inside the remaining egg.

But the pain is unbearable in my dream, too. I cry and whimper as I descend from the nest, then I return to the den within my dream. All I want to do is curl myself up and resist any tension in my muscles because the cramps are awful. It seemed like hours before I could finally fall asleep within my dream.

The pain when I awoke this morning was just as acute as it was in the dream. I agonized throughout the day, but, fortunately, the worst of the spasms didn't start until Julia left the house for the party down the street. If this paroxysm persists, I'll have to return to Grammy's cabin. The pain and the splatter from my guts would be too much for Julia to bear.

I suppose I should leave now, but I really don't want her to wonder where I am. I could leave a note, I suppose, with some lie about why I had to leave for Grammy's cabin. Anything, at this point, would be better than telling her the truth or waiting for an ambulance to show up here if she found me like this and decided to call for medical help.

I had looked so forward to being with Julia today, too. This would've been the first Fourth of July celebration for me here since I left for England a decade ago. I had thought this day might rekindle some purposeful connection for me to America and my place within it here in Kentucky. Instead, it's only underscored how truly isolated I am here, or anywhere for that matter. I am without a country, a native to nothing except for this legacy that has stricken me with an affliction that will surely cause my untimely demise or imprisonment.

I'm starting to fear that the only independence that I'll ever truly know going forward will happen when I finally give myself over to this deranged upheaval to my life that not only is making me absolutely crazy, but also changing me into something that is no longer strictly human.

I was starting to feel like I was on a roll with the good changes in my life. Guess not.

# FRIDAY, JULY 8TH

## "THE FIRE OF ITS SOUL GLOWS FOREVERMORE."

I used to believe that the dead were done with whatever remained alive. It always seemed logical, or maybe just easier, to think that way. There's already such a clutter of information about the dead without the need for another voluminous addition concerning the nature of those who are clearly not with us in the physical sense any longer.

I never had any reason to believe that the dead were anything but dead until recently. Even though I believe that the dead can be alive, or at least undead, it's not like I'm seeing apparitions in broad daylight or anything else of the sort. It is within a dream that is all too real to be only just a dream that I have been visited these past three nights.

Today is Friday, July 8th, as I write this from Grammy's porch. On the first of these nights when I awoke within my dream, I couldn't budge from my fixation upon the unhatched egg in the nest on the bridge above my dream den. Beyond me in the darkened distance, a gust surged from the spot where it felt to me like I used to witness the launch of the Nightmare Eagle that uprooted my apartment building in Rome.

But I couldn't take my eyes off the egg, even when the wind from the distant gust finally reached me to swirl all around me and buffeted the nest itself. In the calm that follows the upheaval of wind, I feel my ears perk at the repeated crunch of snow from the slope below the ridge. I whimper as the crunching steps resound louder and their source draws closer and closer to me.

I don't want to remove my stare from the egg, but I know that I must do so in order to prepare myself for the sight of whatever it is that is coming toward me. I climb down from the egg to gaze beyond the ridge. That's when I see the skeleton walking on two feet toward me. I stand on all fours transfixed as the skeleton hobbles up the slope toward me. In its approach, dots of light flash faster and faster along the skeletal bones until the bones themselves start to retain the pulsating glow.

As the skeleton continues its approach, the throbbing glow starts to darken from opaque matter that seems to stick to the bones. I then detect the scent of blood coming from the skeleton as it gains more and more mass in its approach up the slope. I find my dream body is mesmerized by the sight of internal organs and muscle forming, like the skeleton is dressing itself with life as it nears me.

Next comes the skin, and, when the transfigured entity stands right in front of me, I watch the beard sprout across its completely human face. I thought for sure that this supernatural entity was about to inflict far worse torment upon me than the Nightmare Eagle ever had. But the regenerated man didn't harm me. He merely leaned toward me and spoke.

His message reverberates within me even now. It feels like he's about to speak to me again, loud and clear within my own mind like his words are the only truth of this world and the next. I hear his message again: he tells me that I am a newborn who craves the spirit that will nourish my salvation because I now know what tastes good and what doesn't. He pauses before he resumes to tell me that only a dog return to its own vomit.

That is all he says. That is his message.

After the reborn man said this within my dream, he turned away from me and returned down the slope. I watched him hobble into the distance until I could barely see him. He then turned around toward me and waved at me before he collapsed to the ground and the gust again blew toward me, howling as it raced up the slope to finally meet me and pelt my face with stinging cold.

The eyes of my dream body wouldn't shut, though. I don't think I slept, and when dawn broke, it seemed to me like I was staring ahead from Grammy's porch like I was looking down the darkened, snowy slope where the skeletal man had risen and then collapsed back to nothing.

I went about my day at Grammy's, but it felt like night-time dream had merged into daytime reality. My unalterable stare within the dream seemed like the same stare of my wakefulness. It felt like I was almost catatonic. Only the cramping pain from the blood-thirst interrupted my vacant stare. Fortunately, raw blood liver and oyster crackers quelled the blood-thirst just enough to keep me from suffering even worse.

When the day finally drew to a conclusion, I couldn't wait to finally fall asleep. It seemed like all of my senses had finally shut off when the start of the second dream jolted me awake within my dream. I clambered from the dream den to reach the rock slab of bridge. I scaled the nest to peer inside at the unhatched egg. This time, I did not fixate upon the egg. Instead,

I returned to the bridge to peer down the snowy slope below the ridge where the man had risen.

That's when the gust returned and with its chilled wind brought the skeleton to life again. I watched the same phenomena repeat itself as the skeleton regenerated into human form in its approach up the slope. But as the man came nearer to me, I noticed that this man was a different man than the one from the night before. This man was much larger, his brown beard much fuller and unwieldy, his facial features sharper and more hardened.

When the man reached me, he held his hand to my face and let me sniff him. There was something familiar about him, even though I had no doubt that I'd never seen him before. I licked the back of his hand, and he started to speak, telling me his name–Madoc, Prince of Wales and brother to the most legendary of all earthly kings, Arthur of the Roundtable.

This Madoc entity then told me that he had arrived in this Dark and Bloody Place of Kentucky many moons ago, leading his people from across the great sea to this land of wilderness. He told me that his people prospered here but also drew the aggression of the people who already lived here, causing a war that consumed all of his own and his people's efforts.

Madoc told me of his murder, how he was captured and set on fire, but many of his people survived him to become the people known as the Moon-Eyed. He then told me of the woman witch who raised him from his burnt bone and flesh of ash so that he could transform into the night wolf and return to this wilderness and the remnant of his people, of which I am one.

He was and *is* Madoc the Werewolf, he told me. And I am, he then said, one of his Moon-Eyed people that he calls his lycanthropes. His message fulfilled me somehow. It was like the questions I had about what was happening to me and who I really am were answered. There was a measure of assurance I felt by what this Madoc the Werewolf conveyed to me. My sense of place shifted into a reality that now suddenly subsumed all that was both real and dream.

But Madoc revealed even more for me. He explained that only through the blood-thirst and its derangement could the afflicted one be blessed by both what possessed them and redeemed them. He claimed that the blood-thirst was far from just a murderous feature of my beastly transformation.

No, he said: the blood-thirst has evolved to empower the spirit through which it has passed since its origination. Those with the blood-thirst are chosen to perpetuate a legacy of benevolence, not rapacious mutilation and indiscriminate killing. As much as I found this hard to believe considering my own feasting upon the corpse of the dentist, I still found some measure of truth in what Madoc said because I really did try to bring the crime commited against the dentist to the light of day.

Madoc concluded his address to me with the affirmation that the violence within me was designed to protect me. Its legacy found the "savior" to continue the survival of his people, of which, he reassured me, I was one. He then patted me upon the head before he began his descent of the slope below the ridge. I watched him reach the spot where his skeleton had risen, then he waved to me before the gust blew. Madoc then collapsed back into the snow.

On the third night, Grammy came to visit me in the same skeletal way the first two visitors had. I was disappointed by the brevity of her visit, though. I wanted her to stay and stroke me back to sleep within my dream, but she merely told me to go through with my plans in the daylight and that she would see me once again. She then left without so much as a pat of my head or stroke of my back. I whimpered as I watched her descend the slope and return to the spot from which her skeleton had risen. I howled as loud as I could when I saw her collapse to the ground. I kept howling, even as the gust reached me and whooshed all around me. I howled as loud as I could until the wind subsided.

I knew the dreams were over for now. The forces at work in my transformation had resolved many of the difficulties that I had faced. I knew I was strengthened by these visitations. They affirmed that I was doing exactly what I need to be doing in order to survive individually and ensure that the legacy I was born into would also survive the test of time.

I clambered back to the den to sleep within my dream, knowing I'll pick up Celeste from her grandparents to spend the night with Julia and me as we prepare for our journey across the country to see my mother in Ensenada. There will undoubtedly be a lot of driving involved for both Julia and me, but, hopefully, we'll be energized by the stops we make along the way.

# JULY 13TH

## NORTH PADRE ISLAND, TEXAS

Celeste must think that Julia and I are a couple of real idiots. It's no wonder that the poor little thing broke out in tears tonight at our campsite here. She must've had much higher expectations about our North Padre Island destination than what she encountered today upon our arrival. The beach here with its dunes in this primitive camping area is nice enough, but the water resembles a toilet bowl clouded with diarrhea. Despite her professed reservations about the discolored Gulf of Mexico murk, Celeste entered the water at our encouragement.

There were a few swimmers farther down the beach, but the water conditions where Celeste entered didn't really register for Julia or me. We didn't realize something was wrong until Celeste started screaming and splashing back toward shore. At first, I thought that she had seen a shark or stepped on a jellyfish, so I went splashing into the water after her. That's when Celeste sobbed and pointed at saucer-sized objects that floated everywhere. I took one from the water and considered it: it looked like a stepped-on cow pie; hard, flat, and brown.

Julia surmised that the cow pies were actually some type of oil production waste, maybe related to offshore drilling. This explanation seemed to calm the rattled Celeste. Well, until Celeste ran into her next problem: an infantry of fire ants that reached her and bit her before she could smack them from her bare foot.

Celeste screamed even louder as her cry wailed. Julia plucked her from the sand and whisked her away back to our camp. Julia treated the few ant bites with aloe before the next attack came at dusk in the agency of a veritable squadron of mosquitoes. The attack hit all three of us simultaneously, and we all started to smack ourselves as we jumped around to deter the biting pests. We all three ran for the car. Julia and Celeste dove into the back seat as I flung myself into the driver's seat. I opened the glove box to take out the bottle of mosquito repellant I put there. I applied some to myself before I handed the bottle to Julia, who applied the spray to Celeste first then herself.

Unfortunately, Celeste smeared the chemical into her eyes, causing them to sting so bad that she kept screaming, "My eyes! My eyes!" Julia grabbed a bottle of water from the backseat and doused part of her shirt with it before she dabbed Celeste's eyes with the wet cloth. Julia hugged poor, shuddering Celeste until she finally calmed down.

We thought everything was all right, and it was until we went back to the beach. I had absolutely no idea that crabs would suddenly invade the darkening shore, clacking their claws and scuttling all around us. Celeste screamed so loud as the crabs surrounded us that I instinctively swept her up and ran back to the tent with her in my arms and Julia in pursuit.

When I reached the tent, I asked Julia to take Celeste inside to try to calm her down while I went back to the car. I've been here for a while now. The windows remain up despite the heat because I don't want to risk another round of bites from the mosquitoes. I had the overhead light for so long in order to write all of this that I started the car to make sure the battery wasn't dead.

Now that I've had the opportunity to reconstitute the day, I can only hope that tomorrow is an improvement. At least the tent is pitched near the public restroom so they won't have to squat in the middle of a swarm of mosquitoes and fend off attacking crabs should they need to go to the restroom in the middle of the night. I seriously doubt either of them will want to leave the tent tonight, though. It's about time for me to join them. I just hope we all get enough sleep before the torrid sun bakes the inside of the tent to drive us out for the start of our day.

# JULY 14TH

## SOUTH PADRE ISLAND, TEXAS

The couple of hours required by car to reach this oasis of South Padre Island seemed more like ten minutes after all of the highway travel we've managed thus far. The difference between night and day has revealed the reprieve of this new, paradise of a location.

Evidently the discovery of the lovely South Padre Island is one shared by many. There is a fleet of RVs parked all around us. We've pitched our tent on a hump of grass that is shared by four other campers with tents pitched.

Along the beach, the seaside corridor of multi-storied hotels with whirlpools and cabanas along the shore is a miraculous improvement over stark and cruel North Padre Island. Celeste is having a blast now, like last night's debacle never happened. Julia appears to be in her element here, too. Her mirrored shades framing her subdued visage and her mauve one-piece swimsuit perfectly posturing her supple self.

I excused myself from the beachfront throng after Julia offered to watch Celeste bob in the Gulf of Mexico for a while. I told her that I'd buy more suntan lotion, but I really intended to buy more beef liver. The blood-thirst is starting to double me over again with severe cramps.

Now, that I've returned to the tent and appeased my hunger, I thought I'd take the opportunity to write this, even though sweat drops onto the page as I write these words within the tent. I just hope that the resumption of the blood-thirst isn't a forerunner for my dream to return again. These nights since the new moon have been serene internally in that the dream seems to be smothered. We'll see.

# MONDAY, JULY 18TH

## SANTA MONICA, CALIFORNIA

Julia said that I whimpered and growled as I slept in the backseat during the drive from Palm Springs to Hollywood. I downplayed the significance of that outburst, though, telling Julia that I dreamt I was a dog trying to walk through the smog we had seen when we entered the windmill landscape of Palm Springs. As tired as I was when we witnessed the blackest blanket of ubiquitous smog imaginable, I'm surprised the dream returned, but I'm just glad that nothing I did alarmed Julia or Celeste too much.

As intense as the dream had been in the car, I'm actually surprised that my unconscious reactions to it didn't alarm Julia and Celeste to the point where they woke me up. The dream was more lucid than ever. I was wide awake when I scaled out of the den then tore off downhill into the snow in search of Grammy, only this time I didn't see any tracks to guide me.

My frustrated search continued for some time until I finally decided to return to the den. Once I reached the rock bridge, I leapt to the nest and climbed it. When I saw the solitary unhatched egg amidst the fragments of the broken shells, I pounced upon the egg, attacking it with my teeth and claws in my attempt to break its shell.

That must've been when the whimpers and growls issued from me within the car. I finally gave up on my effort to open the egg and returned to the den, where I once again fell asleep within my dream.

Julia hadn't relayed what she had heard me doing in my dream until she and Celeste returned to the car in Hollywood. The two of them had went to eat at a fast-food restaurant, letting me remain asleep in the backseat. Julia offered to go back to the restaurant when she returned to the car, but I insisted I wasn't hungry. Of course, I didn't qualify that by saying I wasn't hungry for anything cooked.

The pangs of the blood-thirst were even more immediate and severe when I awoke to the view of the rubber mat on the backseat floorboard. Julia asked me if I wanted to drive to Santa Monica from Hollywood. I passed, stating an upset stomach, but it's much worse than that. The stomach constrictions made me cringe, even as I concocted the dream of the dog in the smog for Julia and Celeste. It was all I could do to keep from groaning as I remained as still as I could in the backseat during the drive to Santa Monica. The foam is starting to flow from my mouth without my control over it.

I suppose all of the driving could've exacerbated my affliction. I drove from El Paso, Texas to Palm Springs at night. It was strange to drive through the desert at night. The stretches of absolutely flat land created the hypnotic illusion of bumper-to-bumper traffic based upon the headlights, even though the actual distances between cars was vast.

Julia took over after my turn, and she also had driven to El Paso from San Marcos, where we spent the night at the house of one of her former college roommates. It was there that I agreed to a change of plans that would take us farther north into Southern California rather than going straight to San Diego for our eventual descent along the Baja Coast of Mexico.

Julia and Celeste are on the Santa Monica pier now. I told them my stomach was bothering me too much for me to join them. Writing this has helped a little to take my mind off of my condition, but I'm starting to feel dizzy from the lack of food, bloody raw or otherwise. I try to sip water, but it doesn't neutralize the foam. I've swallowed so much of it now that I think I'd better vomit before they return to the car.

# MONDAY, JULY 18TH

## SAN DIEGO, CALIFORNIA

These are much nicer accommodations than what we had in San Marcos. The house here in San Diego has a hot tub in the sunroom, and the backyard is an in-ground pool. It was a noisy affair when we arrived, as Julia's cousin and his wife have four pre-teenage children who all absolutely adore their Aunt Julia. It was nice to see Celeste immediately embraced by the children. They played together in the pool for a couple of hours before going to bed.

It took everything I had to keep from submitting to total body spasms. I explained to the adults that I must be suffering from a severe bout of car sickness. That seemed understandable enough to them, as they left me to myself on a patio chaise lounge on the pool deck with a wet washcloth over my face. Julia brought me iced tea and told me her cousin had an hors d'oeuvres spread inside. I feebly asked her what they had. I stopped her when she mentioned the pâté and asked what kind of liver it was.

Julia replied that I could join them inside and ask my question, but I once again gave the excuse of car sickness for staying put. She lifted her sunglasses to meet my eyes, which probably shook in their sockets as much as my bones seemed to shiver. She asked me if I were okay. I told her that I just felt really nauseous, but that I would live.

She then finally answered my question about the pâté, saying she didn't know what kind it was but would find out and bring some to me if I wanted. I said pâté sounded perfect to me, especially if I could have some oyster crackers with it. She raised her eyebrow at me then lowered her sunglasses back over her eyes. She leaned to me and kissed my sweaty forehead. My smile quivered in reply as I gripped the sides of the chaise lounge for dear life. I watched her glance back to me in her return to the house, then I covered my face with the washcloth again.

The pâté and oyster crackers did wonders for me. The foam dissipated and my energy restored to a level that enabled me to move without cramping and nausea. I eventually made my way to the hot tub, where I'm now writing this.

Everyone else is inside. I volunteered to sleep outside, even though Julia offered to share her bed with me. I told her I didn't want to wake her up if I felt sick again, but a night of attempted sleep in a patio chaise lounge might make me regret that decision in the morning.

I'm partly afraid of what I'll do when I fall asleep. I'm also charged with the anticipation of seeing my mother again for the first time in a decade. I haven't had correspondence with her in over five years, either, so this is definitely a reunion that's been a long time coming.

We might have more to catch up on than I bargained for, though. She obviously knows more about the legacy Grammy has bequeathed to me than she told me over the phone. Perhaps she shares my affliction. Maybe that's why she's living in Mexico.

I'll have to wait a while longer before we're estranged no more. The drive from here to La Bufadora will take a few hours. Apparently, the ride back could take much longer if the Tijuana traffic is snarled at the border crossing with vehicles leaving Mexico.

Fortunately, Julia and Celeste also have passports, so that should expedite our border passage through Tijuana. Julia said she previously visited Mexico, but I was surprised that Celeste had a passport. Lucinda explained they had planned to take a family trip to England last year. The trip never happened, though, so this is Celeste's first trip out of the country.

I just hope I don't make this a much more eventful trip than it needs to be. I do need to try to sleep some tonight. Perhaps my dream won't keep me awake within my sleep, or worse.

# TUESDAY, JULY 19TH

## MIDNIGHT IN SAN DIEGO, CALIFORNIA

Somehow, I feel, if not purged, then at least validated. My mother appeared quite older than I remembered. There's a serenity about her now that she didn't have before. She seemed pleased with the life where her path has led. Her placidity today exuded like her jasmine perfume and blended with the sea breeze aroma above the intermittently spouting blowhole cliff.

This fragrance soothed me, even as it seemed to subdue the foam from forming in my mouth. The gorgeous vista had to help, too. The ocean at La Bufadora was the deepest blue I've ever seen. The crags and boulders strewn along the shore were the last front to the depth and vastness of the pelagic horizon beyond our perch at the overlook restaurant where my mother and I sat. The ethereal signature we witnessed together would be dotted periodically with an exclamation point every time the wave action forced air to explode a geyser from the top of the cliff.

La Bufadora–the Blowhole.

Celeste shrieked with delight when the ocean spray from the geyser splattered her in its fall from the height above. She seemed to thoroughly enjoy herself today. It's heartening to know that she can find happiness in the things she experiences despite the turmoil that is going on in her life right now.

As for Julia, she also basked in the glow of our environs, even more so as she helped my mother drain a pitcher of margaritas. Those two actually conversed quite freely, which was good to see. Julia did part company from my mother to take Celeste to the blowhole rock for a while, so that my mother and I could speak privately.

That's when the conversation between my mother and me turned dramatically. She immediately asked me how much I suffered from my peculiar thirst and diet. I had traveled too far to lie to my mother, but I only mentioned to her that I had acquired an unusual appetite for raw beef liver. My mother then informed me what we both already knew—that Grammy also suffered from the blood-thirst. She then explained Grammy's condition to me in clinical terms, adding that the affliction is hereditary—a genetic message that alters everything, or so it seems.

My mother said she herself did not suffer from the blood-thirst, then she detailed what Grammy would do during awakened hours to alleviate some of the discomfort that the symptoms caused. I already knew that Grammy ate the oyster crackers to soothe her throat scorched from radiation treatments. I also knew that Grammy liked the crackers because teeth weren't required to eat them: she could suck them, then easily swallow the cracker paste. I had obviously already discovered that the crackers dissolve the hydrophobic paste, but my mother confirmed for me that Grammy also ate the crackers for this reason, as well.

Once it became clear to me that we were on the same page of the affliction, my mother shifted the subject to the derangement that accompanies my condition. She confirmed that Grammy periodically suffered from the derangement. She didn't specifically mention the transformation, which meant that Grammy might have spared my mother from the encounter with an actual werewolf.

My mother then described how she would help Grammy prepare for the imminent derangement by securing Grammy to the hanging hooks within the smokehouse behind the cabin. My mother insisted that she never went into the smokehouse when she heard the growls and howls emanate from its interior. She said she did this quite frequently over the years, but she couldn't help Grammy quarantine herself once she married my late father. She worried that Grammy might have had something to do with some of the reports she heard and read about when she wasn't able to help Grammy. Those reports involved murders and mutilated bodies.

I really wish that Julia could have heard the conversation between my mother and me. I hope that my mother somehow steered the conversation between her and Julia in that direction during my absence. It hasn't come up between Julia and me since we parted company with my mother, but my whole derangement issue is bound to show itself, so to speak, sooner or later.

Now that I've spent my time with my mother, it's time for Julia and me to drive back home to Kentucky. Our plan is to return to South Padre island first, though. It wasn't part of our original plan, but Julia and Celeste all loved the placed so much. We have the time to spend a day and night there on the way back.

The only problem with that plan, however, is that we won't

make it back to the confines of Grammy's property before the full moon wreaks its havoc upon me. I already abhor what I'm about to do. Regardless of what happens, I'm encouraged by the reunion between my mother and me. The family affliction wasn't the only topic of our conversation. As much as my mother had clearly prioritized telling me all that she knew about the affliction, she was overwhelmed to tears when I introduced Celeste as her granddaughter. Of course, it took some time for me to explain to my mother about the whole sordid affair between Lucinda and me and what is happening between Lucinda and Herschel now.

I'm just so glad that my mother had the chance to meet her granddaughter, and that Celeste met her grandmother. I hope those two will meet again someday and perhaps spend significantly more time together. If that's the only good that's come of all of this, so be it.

# THURSDAY, JULY 21ST

## SOUTH PADRE ISLAND

The dazzle of gold points of light that flash all about her unworldly face presage the hatch of my looming fate. The haunt is here. I peripherally detected the anomaly at first, and it was just enough of a visual aberration to warrant a glance in the direction of her bizarre sparkle.

When I focused my attention upon the sparkling phenomenon, the points of light aligned themselves upon her glowing profile for my accursed eyes alone to see.

When she turned her face toward me, blood churned through me like it wanted to pound its way through my skin. The foamy drool then spilled down my chin and slathered my face.

Her violet eyes beamed the future to me. The seemingly same scant string bikini top that she wore at the Red River Gorge hoisted her goddess bosom for me to devour with my eyes, but, somehow, I stayed strangely at ease, as though our meeting again was so ordained that its destiny fused with my very marrow.

For her part, she just seemed to look right past me without so much as a blink of recognition. The Girl from Ohio with her violet eyes has done just what she said she would do. She's here at South Padre Island some three months after she left her note for me atop Moonshiner's Arch at the Gorge. She's here now for my sake, whether she realizes this or not. She is more than just a messenger from Grammy, or whoever, or whatever, is responsible for my grueling affliction.

Beardless and barbered, I am no doubt incognito, as far as she is concerned. Soon, I will reveal myself to her. The outcome of this rendezvous then can reveal itself to me. I'm far too imbued with gore now to turn back from the encounter ahead. There is the expulsion of an entire genetic composition to consider in all of this. It is the legacy of who I am, or what I am. This vortex that joins us is hers and mine alone.

I really don't want to offend Julia. Her presence beside me was strong enough to keep me from approaching the Girl from Ohio the moment I saw her. Hopefully Julia will never have to know what is about to happen between the Girl from Ohio and me. I couldn't expect Julia to understand the nature of this bestial attraction.

The Girl from Ohio left her tent intact before she and her female friend traipsed away from the campground mound. Since then, Julia has taken Celeste to the beach, but they'll have to return before much longer. It's almost nightfall now. I've been alone here in the car for far too long. I might just sleep here, though, feigning recurrent stomach turbulence as my reason for not sleeping in the tent with Julia and Celeste. I'm afraid I'd scare the hell out them tonight, one way or another, if I stayed in there with them.

But I doubt there's any way I'll be sleeping tonight. I have more than enough energy to walk as far as I can along the beach in the dark. I don't want Julia to think that I'm pawning Celeste off on her, but if Julia objects to my wish to walk the beach alone at night, I'll insist that I have to do it to help me with the nausea I feel right now.

Physically moving my body does seem to minimize the cravings, except when the spasms are so internally severe that breathing and walking makes for a difficult combination. The onset of darkness has seemed to intensify the internal grumblings that always lead to cramps. The paste is thickening, too, despite the fact that I've eaten a pack of oyster crackers since I started writing this. I suppose I should eat another pack before Julia and Celeste return. I don't have any raw beef liver available, but I suspect that beef liver won't appease my blood-thirst tonight.

## JULY 26TH

### GRAMMY'S CABIN

This place isn't deranged at all. It's just what it has always been for however long it has existed. It's dark here now, but that makes no difference to me at this point. The moonlight is more than enough illumination for me to see what I'm doing. I could even write this here on the porch if clouds completely blocked the moonlight. These are the remains of my affliction.

I doubt that I'll ever be able to recover from whatever has made them such. There's no rehab or retreat for this. At least I can be somewhat content in the knowledge that I didn't damage and maim too much in the midst of my unholy transformation. That's all I can have in the way of redemption.

I have reached the realm of facts where it is obvious that all precautions and remedies fail in the face of normalcy. I'm in a region of wounds. These wounds can be licked, I suppose, but my tongue can't reach my brain or whatever it is that renders me such a monstrosity.

I can't scratch the noise from my ears, either. Even the slightest sound pricks my ears now.

There seems to be some kind of leash fashioned from the fibers of my internal transformation, and it's collared to a world within a dream. All of the other barriers and restraints of any other world are all swept away in the torrent that courses through me. The blood flowed from her and swept me away in its flood as I lapped as much of it up as I could at the trough of the werewolf damned.

I am too alive for this world.

I know what all of this means, even if I'm not completely sure what happened.

I do know that the Girl from Ohio awaited me at the beach, where we had met the previous night. Only, I was so disoriented I had no idea what was happening when I saw that it was her. I opened my eyes in my dream to the sting of saltwater and the rush of the waxing tide. She stumbled over top of my inundated body, and she seemed as helpless as me to orient herself.

Water spewed from my mouth as I choked. Her mouth wouldn't operate correctly as she brought her face to mine. She swayed above me and continued to slur, even as she squatted over me then straddled my stomach. She definitely knew who I was, though. Maybe she thought I was drowning, and maybe I really was because it sure seemed to me like I had fallen asleep on the beach before the tide surged into shore.

I had just emerged from the dream when she found me. It merged with reality in the most amazing way. I was watching the unhatched egg as its shell began to crack. I felt sapped of all energy as the fragments of shell fell to the bottom of the nest. I thought I was about to die when she emerged from the egg: it was the Girl from Ohio.

I was confused by the water that rose from the nest, lifting

her to me at the top of the nest. That's the instant when I mate-
rialized directly from the dream into the reality of our situation
at South Padre Island beach. Her violet eyes glowed as she
hovered above me, and the points of gold light sparkled from her
darkened face.

All that I could do was gurgle and gasp within her mouth
until she pulled her mouth away from mine. She then started to
feebly smack my chest, as though she were flailing just to keep
herself conscious. When she stopped smacking my stomach, she
slumped forward with her head hanging down. I strained to lift
my hand and move her hair from her eyes. Just as I did, I saw
her violet eyes close, then she collapsed onto me with her bare
breasts spreading across my face.

She seemed impervious to my violent spasms beneath her as
the structure of my chest started to change. I howled with pain
into her breasts, shaking my head with each outburst as the tide
rolled more and more into both of us. The sinking sand was
swallowing me, especially more so now with her full weight on
top of me. Between the excruciating pain of my chest twisting
itself into a new shape and the fear of drowning while it was
happening, I thought I was dying one way or another.

The saltwater found its way between her breasts and into
my mouth, forcing me to retch as I howled and snarled and
started to dig at her back with my shapeshifting hands. My
clench upon her tightened as the spasms worsened, the water
crashed into us harder, and the fingers and fists inside me felt
like they were trying to poke and punch their way through my
skin.

The Girl from Ohio finally revived from my violence
beneath her and the waves breaking against us. But instead of
getting up, she tried to match my intensity beneath her by undu-
lating and grinding her lower body against me. She then lunged

to bring her mouth to mine and thrust her tongue into my mouth. She pulled her tongue out of my mouth just as I chomped into her bottom lip. She then shoved my shoulders farther into wet sand, groaning in her struggle to free her imbalanced head from my teeth clenched to her bottom lip.

When she finally did free her lip from my teeth, blood spilled from her mouth. She opened her violet eyes long enough to glimpse me through the exploding surf. She then closed her eyes again, wincing as she drew her tongue across her torn lip.

I desperately groped her to free myself from her and the sinking sand. I saw her smile, and her subsequent moan shrilled to a squeal before she straddled me and pounded my groin with her bare backside so hard and fast that I felt myself pile driven even deeper into the frothy shore.

Despite my predicament and her apparently orgasmic intent, the blood from her lip crazed me into such a frenzy that I growled as I tore at her sides and back in my desperation to quench the blood-thirst. All I wanted was her blood, and when she pinned my shoulders back and slung her mouth over mine, I gulped what gushed from her lip. She then bit my cheek as she shifted her bottom against me so that she could grind herself against me even harder.

Her bite hurt and added to my overall physical agony. I was too intent on the seepage of her blood into my mouth to pry her teeth from my face. As I drank her blood, I burst from the power that flowed through me. I howled louder and more inhumanely than I ever had, then all of the fingers and fists poking and punching inside me simultaneously broke through my skin.

My back arched beyond my ability to control it, lifting all but my shoulders and lower body from the sinking sand, despite the weight of the Girl from Ohio on top of me. The water further buoyed my back, which burst into convulsion so fast and fierce that I thought I might explode. I thought she was about to explode, too, from the sheer rapturous shrieks that escaped from her in her orgasmic release as she dug her nails into my chest.

The water flooded my face, drowning my howl, but it also washed away the slobber of foam from my mouth. She released her bite from my cheek and pushed her top half from my shoulders so that her full weight now crammed against my convulsive groin. She then screamed as shrill and loud as I had howled before she went limp and slumped forward to me, knocking her forehead against mine in her final release.

I squirmed to free myself from her without sinking back into the hollow of sunken sand below my back. As the water brought more wet sand to fill the void beneath me, I finally did nudge her from me. She rolled off me then went splat into the surf and wet sand. Face first and unconscious, the Girl from Ohio would drown and die if I didn't do something to save her. As much as I wanted to shred the flesh from her and lap the blood from the hollow of her chest, I resisted the urge.

I scanned the beach but saw no one near us. I knew it was up to me whether she lived or died. I tried to grab a mouthful of her hair and drag her, but to no avail. Her hair kept slipping through my teeth. I then bit into her arm and clamped down as I backed on all fours toward the dry fringe of the shore. The blood from her arm gushed into my mouth, and I released my bite to lap up as much of her blood as I could before I realized what I was doing.

I clambered around her and bit into her other arm, then I resumed dragging her across the froth of surf and wet sand. Her blood from the fresh bite wound flowed down my throat, seemingly empowering me even more to drag her faster as I backpedaled on all fours. When I did reach dry sand beyond the reach of the tide, I dropped her arm. I saw how badly I had damaged her from my bite.

She remained on her back as I lapped as much blood from the wound as I could. More and more blood flowed from her wounds. She started to retch uncontrollably, gagging then spewing spouts of water. I realized I had to turn her over, so I quit lapping up her blood and shoved my snout into her side. She half opened her unfocused eyes as she tried to lift her head to see me. I pushed until she rolled over to her stomach.

She tried to push herself from the dry sand, but she lacked the strength to offset her wounded arms and otherwise depleted condition. She soon gave up and dropped her face into the dry sand. I went to her one last time, watching the blood from her arms stain the sand around them. I went to her face and licked her twice. She mumbled and twitched.

As much as I wanted to help her, I had done all that I could. Her blood slaked my thirst as, I believe, only hers could. If I stayed any longer beside her, I have no doubt that I would have bitten her more and emptied her of all of her blood.

I could now see some people running toward us, so I fled from her, racing on all fours along the beach in the direction toward my campsite and car. I tore past groups along the beach, hearing their gasps and yells as I neared the campground. I veered around RVs and the smattering of those sitting outside of them, again dodging contact with them as they screamed and shouted. I raced as fast as I could to reach my own campsite as stealthily as I could.

When I finally did find my car on the hump of campground grass, I crawled beneath it and panted horribly to the point I thought that my sides would split open and my lungs explode out of my mouth. Slowly my breathing calmed. I remained as still and silent as I could, waiting for the purple darkness of dawn to come.

I don't know if I fell asleep or not, but I felt a twinge that made it seem like I was awakened. That's when I looked at myself to discover that I was, indeed, myself again. Despite my recovery, I was far too weak to move, so I just waited naked, bruised, and battered beneath the car. I heard sirens blaring in the distance toward the site of my rendezvous with the Girl from Ohio. All I could do was whimper.

Finally, the morning light flooded around me, and the stirring of campers began. I heard my tent unzip and saw Julia, then Celeste crawl out. I heard them discuss my absence, then Celeste offered to check to see if I was in the car. As she peered into the car, my leg twitched bad enough from a cramp in my calf to create a noise. I watched poor little Celeste dig her knees into the ground beside the car, then she lowered her cocked head into my view.

As soon as our eyes met, she sprang up and ran back to Julia. I heard her unsteady whisper for Julia to go to the car and look beneath it. Julia did just that, but she reacted much more demonstrably to my unlikely presence there. She screamed and recoiled from the car at the sight of me. I thought for sure that was it for me.

But it wasn't. I perked my ears as I heard the unflapping of a tent and the voice of a man from a nearby tent ask if she was all right. To my relief, Julia replied that she had nearly stepped on some fire ants. That seemed to satisfy the curiosity of those within earshot of her scream.

Julia's second glance at me came with a chilling scowl, but I averted her stare in my attempt to crawl out from beneath the car. Julia gripped my arm to help me into the open air. She then opened the passenger door and helped me to crawl into the backseat. Once I managed to climb into the backseat, Julia slammed the door shut. In my exhaustion, all I could do was sleep, despite the heat starting to beat down and the agony of my physical condition.

I awoke with a towel over my waist. Julia was already in the process of disassembling the tent with Celeste standing nearby her. A pair of swim trunks were beside me. I put them on.

As I got out of the car, Celeste looked at me, but Julia did not. I went over to Julia and helped her with the tent. No one said anything at the campground or in the car. When I lowered the mirrored visor on the passenger side, I realized the extent of my ghastliness. There was dried blood all over my face, and my cheek was gashed open with what were clearly bite marks.

It was a long ride from South Padre Island to Dallas. Shortly after we took off, Celeste wordlessly handed a jug of water and a towel to me. I cleaned my face and some of my chest, which was speckled and streaked with blood splatter, too.

Julia and I switched at Dallas. I managed to drive to Memphis. Still, no one said much, and Julia slept some in the passenger seat. I finally couldn't keep my eyes open any longer, so I pulled off the highway onto the shoulder. That's when I nudged her awake, which clearly displeased her. She just glared at me with hateful eyes, but I told her that she would have to drive now.

I did doze off a couple of times during her drive to Knoxville. I drove the rest of the way home from Knoxville, then I dropped Julia off at her house. She kissed Celeste on the cheek then told her goodbye. She took her bags from the trunk and silently marched away from me without any acknowledgement. It's clear that what we had is over now. Nothing I can say would change that. There's no way I can explain to her what has happened to me. Plus, I can't risk any more than I've already risked. I'm going to have to plan how I will be able to remain undetected.

After I dropped off Julia, I took Celeste to her grandparents' house. She couldn't wait to get away from me either. Looks like my cameo as a father turned out to be a major bust. At least, she waved goodbye when her grandparents opened the door. I waved back from the car, then took off for Grammy's.

I'm just fearful that the refuge here is ruined. I have no idea what Celeste will tell her grandparents or her mother. I have no idea if Julia will share the details of my condition in South Padre Island with anyone. Her disclosure could lead to questioning by authorities.

As much as I'd like to just take some money and drive as far away as possible, I can't physically do that right now. My body is one big ache with wounds that I suppose I'll still have to treat, even though I'm a lycanthrope now.

So, I'll just have to bide my time here for a day or two while I figure out what to do next.

Or maybe I'm already too late.

I heard what sounded like a pickup truck stop on the road. One door opened then shut. I guess I'll find out who my visitor is directly, but I suspect it might be Herschel. We'll see.

# WEDNESDAY, JULY 27TH

## GRAMMY'S CABIN

I thought Herschel would be my visitor yesterday. Maybe I just hoped that it would be him, so that I could know Herschel was alive and free after his incident with Lucinda. Turns out it wasn't Herschel: it was Virgil, my sporting goods buddy from Winchester.

Apparently, Virgil has taken a substantial interest in how things turn out for me. Based upon how he has treated me so far, I'd have to say his interest is genuine, which is something I welcome. As much as I wanted to get up and greet Virgil as he approached Grammy's cabin, I just couldn't get out of the chair. I remained on the porch and awaited his arrival, instead.

Of course, he wanted to know about my gashed face and my bare, clawed chest. I told him he really didn't want to know, but that the perpetrator was the wildest woman I ever met.

Our conversation after that became quite relaxed. Virgil took a seat on the porch and remained there for the next few hours. The more we talked, the more obvious it became to me that he wanted to help me more than he already had. He clearly understood that I was in the kind of trouble that is so deep that it takes considerable effort and extended time to figure out exactly what to do next.

When I told him that it wasn't wise for me to stay at Grammy's much longer, he offered for me to join him for his drive tomorrow to Tellico Lake in Tennessee near Knoxville, where he owned some property and was headed to look at a bait store and tackle shop that he might buy.

There really isn't anything for me here now anyway, other than this property. Virgil and I even talked about me selling the place here. That way I could just cash out and split for good. The appeal of making a fresh start is very strong. It might be the only way that I can escape detection or at least prolong my freedom. I'm afraid my future might very well be a series of moves before somebody figures out what kind of fugitive I am and tries to stop me.

I stopped short of telling Virgil that I'm a lycanthrope, though. Still, he seems to sense that there's something about me that's considerably different than most. I did relate my dream to him, not the Nightmare Eagle part of it, but the wolf dream of the den and the natural bridge. Turns out my description of the dream locale bore a considerable resemblance to an actual place Virgil knew in Kentucky. The One-Wagon-Wide Bridge is what he called it. He said we'll make a stop there tomorrow on our way to Tellico Lake.

Sounds like the closest thing to a plan that I have working right now. There's really nothing left for me to tend to here now. I'll just lock up the cabin and go for as long as I'm gone. I'll sort out the sale of Grammy's property later, if that's what I have to do.

There is the matter of all of this writing, though. I mainly wanted to write to remember where I was and what I was becoming. I suppose all that I've written definitely incriminates me. I could just burn these notebooks here or hide them somewhere on the property. But part of me feels like I need to keep all of this for some reason. I could always explain away the content as material for a book I'm writing, if I were apprehended and the notebooks confiscated. Regardless, this last notebook is almost full. I have enough room for one more entry tomorrow, so I'll sleep on this decision about what to do with the notebooks.

As for Virgil, he headed back to Winchester. He'll pick me up bright and early tomorrow, so I suppose I need to figure out what I'm taking with me on this road trip. One thing I know I'll have with me for sure is one hell of an affliction.

# THURSDAY, JULY 28TH

## ONE-WAGON-WIDE BRIDGE

I shuddered when I saw the bridge. It was the exact same slab of natural rock bridge that I dreamed over and over again during my transition into the lycanthrope.

I also couldn't believe my eyes when I surveyed the valley on the other side of the ridge. Even though there was no snow, I knew this was exactly the same valley down which I would pursue Grammy's trail in my dream.

Virgil told me about the bridge history and legend of the two brothers who fought over the right to its passage. As interesting as the history was, I couldn't hardly wait to climb down to the ledge where I knew my dream den was located.

Virgil advised against climbing down, though. He said it was too dangerous.

I said I really needed to climb down to see if the ledge below the bridge matched the den in my dream. He said he had some rope with which I could repel down, but that this would still be dangerous because he didn't actually have repelling equipment with him.

I said I'd take the risk if he could come up with the material and lower me down. When he said he could, that's when it struck me what to do with all of these notebooks. If this place wasn't readily accessible, then someone would need a damn good reason to climb down to what would be considered an insignificant place by virtually all standards.

When I mentioned to Virgil that I might like to collect some rocks or other material from the ledge, he offered me the use of a backpack he had in the pickup bed. He showed me the backpack then excused himself to take a leak in the woods. I had already bundled my four note-books within sheets of aluminum foil after I decided to not to burn them. I put the notebook bundle into the backpack during his absence, then I slipped into the backpack.

Virgil returned, saying we did need to do this quickly so we could hit the road. I promised I'd be quick. He grabbed the fifty feet of rope he had, and we went to the bridge. He tied the rope to the tree nearest the bridge, then I ran the other end of the rope through the belt loops of my shorts.

Virgil told me to wait while he went back for a pair of gloves. I assessed how I would descend while he was gone. When he returned with the pair of rawhide gloves, I put them on. He also wore a pair. He gripped the rope behind me as I stepped into position to start my descent.

With Virgil above me and the rope knotted to the tree, I felt as assured as I could be that I was safe, despite the sheer drop below me. I climbed slowly, securing my footing and using my gloved fingers to gain handholds.

I climbed all the way down until I reached the ledge. There was no doubt that this place was my dream den. Everything I dreamed was still guiding me now. I hollered up to Virgil that he could take a break so that I could look around for about ten minutes and gather what I wanted to take back.

I soon found the ideal place to hide my notebooks. I brushed away the heap of rubble at the base of the ledge where it featured a slight overhang. I soon realized that I wasn't the first person to hide something here. I uncovered a small wooden box with an item inside of it that I didn't understand: a small rectangular rock with some kind of inscription in a language I had never seen. I pocketed the box and rock, then I unbundled the notebooks to write this final entry in the last notebook.

I'm now about to stash the notebook bundle within the space I had cleared. Virgil called down to me just then, and I told him that I'd be coming up in a minute. I've grabbed a few other interesting rocks to put in the backpack so I can study them later.

But for now, this is the end.

# ABOUT THE AUTHOR

Robb Hoff writes novels that test the boundaries of reality. *Crackers For The Lycanthrope* is the harrowing prequel of Robb Hoff's The Lycanthrope horror series that began with the occult odyssey of *Contract With The Lycanthrope*.

Hoff is also author of the Eggsquisite Corpse Thriller series that features the Salvador Dali-inspired *CosmicEgg Rapture* and relentless supernatural thriller *Serpent Egg Rapture*. Both of his series are published by Hydra Publications.

ALSO BY ROBB HOFF


*COSMIC EGG RAPTURE*

*SERPENT EGG RAPTURE*

*CONTRACT WITH THE LYCANTHROPE*